Romance: Billionaire Box Set

Jodi Cooper

Copyright © 2014

Published by Run Free Publishing

All rights reserved.

No part of this publication may be reproduced, stored in a retrieval system, or transmitted, in any form or by any means without the prior permission in writing of the publisher.

This romantic collection includes these titles:

Romance: The Billionaire Boss

Romance: Interviewing the Billionaire

Romance: The Billionaire Actor

Romance: The Billionaire's Assistant

Romance: The Billionaire's Mansion

Romance: Secret Billionaire

Plus bonus story:

Romance: Bad Boy Biker

Romance: The Billionaire Boss

Jodi Cooper

Copyright © 2014

Published by Run Free Publishing

All rights reserved.

No part of this publication may be reproduced, stored in a retrieval system, or transmitted, in any form or by any means without the prior permission in writing of the publisher.

Romance: The Billionaire Boss

Chapter 1

Today is the first day in my new role as a personal assistant to the boss of the biggest investment firm on this side of the country.

The firm has an amazing reputation, based on years of making money for its exclusive clients. However Mr Joel Hill, my new Billionaire boss, has a different reputation. We all know that he is prick. He treats people like shit, and then expects them to turn over backwards for him. He asks his personal assistants to tie his shoe laces while he's in the elevator, and he demands that they bring him coffee at all hours of the night. He makes ridiculous requests for lunch and he demands that everyone leaves the gym when he arrives. He's a prick. Maybe that's why he's so successful in running this business.

But he also has the reputation of looking after his employees. Although the average lifespan of a personal assistant to Mr Hill is only six months, the last woman who held the job did so for a year and a half.

When she handed in her registration, he bought her a mansion by the beach in Florida as a way to say thankyou. She could sell that house and be set up for life.

So I have a goal. Work eighteen months for the worst boss and be set-up for life. Eighteen months is all I have to last.

And it's not like there are no other perks to this job.

Mr Joel Hill is good to look at. He is always dressed in the best tailored suits, fitted to his strong, muscular physique. Rumour is that he travels to Italy just to get his suits fitted. And then to France just to get his hair cut.

His tall, dominant statue stands over most people and his face is Hollywood beautiful.

Then there are his eyes. I could become lost in those deep, blue eyes.

When I creep into his office first thing in the morning, he is standing at the window, looking out on the world below. I place the daily schedule folder on the edge of his desk and he doesn't move. I take a moment to admire his broad shoulders.

"Are you the new personal assistant?" his voice is deep and governing.

"Yes," I reply nervously.

He finally turns around. His eyes judge me. He looks me up and down, judging my stance, my clothes and my overall look.

"Your name?"

"Amy Robinson, Mr Hill."

"No, please call me Joel. We will be getting to know each other very well over the next few months, so you need to call me Joel."

I nod in obedience.

"Are you very worldly, Amy?"

"Worldly? Um… yes," I lie. I'm not worldly. I'm only recently out of college, and college was the quiet life for me. There were no wild parties or college orgies, and there was barely a boyfriend over the last few years.

My worldly experience is limited.

"Really?" he questions me.

"I've travelled a bit. I spent six months travelling through Asia."

"No, no. I don't mean travel. I mean," he pauses, "Have you experienced life?"

"Um... yes. I think so."

"I don't think so, Amy."

"You don't think so?"

"You look too innocent to understand how the world works. The world works on a give and take principle, Amy. If you've got something to give, then someone else is happy to take it. I can see that you have something to give."

"And what do I have to give?"

"Your looks."

I am a little taken a back.

"I haven't had an assistant as innocent as you before. I always ask for a personal assistant that is attractive and experienced in the way the world works. All my previous assistants have been quite worldly. I'm disappointed that you're not worldly. At least you fit the first category. But I'm not going to send you back. I would like to teach you about give and take."

"Ok."

"Ok?" he questions.

I nod.

"It's not just ok. You have to be all in. You can't be half-in in this job. You are the personal assistant to one of the richest men in the country.

I will treat you like dirt and you have to love it. You have to be committed. Are you committed?"

I swallow nervously, "Yes. I want you teach me."

"I like that. I like that you're innocent and you want me to teach you."

"I want you to teach me everything you know," I say, not really knowing what I am getting myself into.

"Then let me hear you say that you're committed."

"I am committed," my voice is shaky.

He takes another look out the window, pauses, and then walks over to me, standing tall and dominant in-front of me. He reaches out and one of his strong hands runs down the side of my face, as he looks deep into my eyes. He pushes my hair back over my ear with a strong finger.

"Good. You are now free to go," he points towards the office door.

Oh wow.

I leave the office with my heart in my mouth – what have I gotten myself into?

"You're the new personal assistant?" a pleasant, older lady asks me in the elevator.

"I'm Joel's new personal assistant, yes."

"Good luck," she whispers. It's strange that she whispered as we are the only two people in the lift.

"Good luck?" I question.

She pauses, fixes her glasses and then holds out her hand, "I'm Melissa. I work in accounts on the 35th floor."

"Amy," I smile.

"Have you finished working with him for today?" her hand is warm and her demeanour is welcoming.

"I have. I'm just on my way out."

"Then let me take you out for coffee, dear. We can have a chat. I'll word you up about some of his many habits. It'll give you the inside running on doing a great job."

"That would be nice. Thanks."

I almost expected everyone who works in Joel's office to be like Joel. Cold-hearted and driven solely by money – so I am pleasantly surprised to see that they are not.

As we walk to the coffee shop next to our building, Melissa begins to explain her working background, "I used to work closely with Joel and I've been with this company since it started. He's certainly taken it a long way from where it used to be. I wasn't his personal assistant but I was his personal accounts manager."

"You don't do that role anymore?"

"Oh no, dear. He's... intense."

"How intense?"

"Very intense. He'll call you up at all hours of the night and asks you questions that you can't possibly answer without getting out of bed and turning on your computer."

"What's he doing thinking about work at all hours of the night?"

"That's all he does, dear. That's all he thinks about. He has no real friends and no real social life. You won't see him in the social pages of a magazine or walking into the office with a fancy girlfriend. No, no – that's not him. All he is about is work."

"Does he have family?"

"Not a family of his own. His mother and father have passed but he still has some aunties and uncles who look out for him."

We sit down to coffee and I notice that Melissa hasn't stopped smiling since we meet, "Are you always this happy? You haven't stopped smiling since you said hello."

"He's going to really like you," she looks at me knowingly.

"Why do you say that?"

"You're his type. You're innocent good looks will suck him in."

"Really?"

"Oh yes. But don't try to get to close too quickly. He'll only push you away if he thinks that you are beginning to like him. He doesn't like emotions – they scare him."

"But he likes money."

"Yes – he likes money. Money is something that he can control. He has complete control over how much money he makes. But he has no control over his emotions. And that really scares him. He loves to be in control."

"He has a reputation of treating his personal assistants like dirt. Is that true?"

"Unfortunately, it is. I think it all comes back to control. He loves to be in command and loves to be the one pulling the strings. When he first started this company, he had investors coming at him from everywhere.

They were drawn to his passion for business but he didn't want anything to with them. It was his company and he runs it his way.

"And just last month, he gave up a deal that would guarantee him ten million dollars a year for ten years because he didn't want someone else to have say in the way he runs the business. Investors are always coming to him – either wanting to buy out the whole business or just to be a small part of the business but he always says no."

"Wow. He really does want complete control. How much do you think he's worth?"

"I work on his personal accounts so I know exactly how much he is worth."

"And how much is that?"

"I can't say, it's his private matter."

"Not even a ball park figure?"

"Well, a magazine last month listed him as a two billion dollar man."

"And were they right?"

"They under-estimated his wealth."

"Wow. That's a lot of money. What would he do with all that cash?"

"It's not cash that he can just draw upon. A lot of it is paper money – the sort that is tied up in investments. Having said that, he can have whatever he wants whenever he wants it."

"I'm impressed."

"Don't be too impressed and don't let the money blind you. That's what happens to a lot of personal assistants to Joel. They get caught up in the money. And as soon as they do that, they're gone. What Joel wants is someone who'll like him for him. He hasn't found that person yet."

"The last girl stayed awhile. Eighteen months, I hear."

"She did. But I didn't like her. I could see through her right away. She was very pretty and wore very sexy clothing to work, but she only ever cared about the money. Which for Joel was good, because that meant that he didn't have to deal with any emotional baggage that might come with a girl like that."

"If she was good, why did he get rid of her?"

"She asked him to marry her."

"What?!" I almost sip out my hot coffee.

"Yes, it's true. After she proposed, he said he'll sell the business and they could spend the rest of their days donating time and money to charity. He was only joking, of course, but he said he never saw a more disgusted look on a girl's face in his life. He knew then that she didn't want him, she only wanted the money and the lifestyle."

"Joel seems nice. If he wasn't the boss, and he wasn't worth all that money, I would ask him out."

"Really?" Melissa's smile grows.

"I don't want to overstate it, but he seems really great. Without the money, I think he would be amazing. He's very charming, very good looking and there seems to be… I don't know, almost a spark between us."

Melissa smiles to herself, stands and places a hand on my shoulder,

"Go for it. But I'll warn you – keep an open mind."

And with a wink, Melissa leaves her half-drunk coffee behind.

After two weeks working for Joel, he invites me into his office at five o'clock for a glass of wine. I nervously agree – I can tell this won't just be a glass of wine.

"Do you like working for me, Amy?"

"Yes," I state as I sip at the delicious wine.

"Good. I like having you work for me."

He comes close to me and invades my personal space. Before I know it, he leans forward and kisses my lips, sending shivers dance through-out my body.

Wow.

His kiss is soft and tender, but I am too shocked to really enjoy this moment.

He draws away and looks me deep in the eyes. Wow.

"Service me," he states firmly, looking away.

"Sorry?" I am surprised.

"Service me," he demands.

He grabs my hand and leads it to his groin, where I feel a large bugle in his grey suit pants.

"Service you? In the office?" I ask.

He nods, "You are a very beautiful woman. I need you to service me. I can't go another day with your gorgeous looks walking though the office. I need your help. You are so stunning."

His eyes look back, deep into mine, almost touching my soul.

Suddenly, I feel under his spell. His dashing looks and charm have me smitten. There's no doubt about that. He could do whatever he wants with me now.

And he does.

He pulls my hair back and starts kissing me on the neck.

"A beautiful woman..." he continues, "With a beautiful personality."

He smoothly lifts the jumper and shirt off my torso, and quickly unclips my bra as he continues to kiss my skin. Before I know it, I am topless. I feel exposed as he starts to kiss my perky breasts.

He begins to sing softly as he kisses all my body and I am lost in his passion. His kisses are so tender and seductive. I can feel the passion in each one of his kisses.

The room is alight with chemistry.

His hands reach around and unzip my skirt, and then he bends down, kissing my legs tenderly.

Before I know it, somehow, I am completely naked in the office of my Billionaire boss.

As soon as I am completely naked, he stops and wanders over to his music player, turning on soft jazz music for the background.

"Dance for me."

"Sorry?"

"Dance for me."

I stand, naked, and begin to dance softly. Joel takes a position on an armchair at the side of the office, watching me. I dance gently as he pulls down his suit pants and jocks down, exposing the lower half of his body. His hand reaches down and he begins to rub his large and long manhood.

"Yes," he half-moans, "Keep dancing."

As the pace of the music quickens, so does my dancing. His eyes are locked onto my naked body, rubbing himself harder when I dance harder.

"Sing my name," he demands.

"Ooohhh Joel," I sing with the music, uncomfortably.

He moans loudly, smoothing his hand over his member. He turns the music up with the remote and I become lost in the moment. His smile makes me forget that I am in an office with a man that I have only just meet, and I escape to a world full of confidence.

Oh, yes.

I dance around the room and then I bend forward, exposing my pussy to his full view, and he stands up. I wiggle my behind in-front of him.

He is beating his member when I turn back around.

"Keep dancing."

I swirl around the room and his eyes follow me the whole way.

"Now rub yourself."

I rub my pussy, exposing myself to him. My heart rate rises as I watch him beat himself. He is so large and long. I moan as I push my fingers inside myself, still standing up. I pump my fingers into and out of myself, squirting juice as I come. I am so wet.

"Jerk me off," he demands.

I walk across and move around the back of him. I place my hand on his heavy member and begin rubbing up and down. It pulsates with my rubbing and feels so strong. He moans and moves his hand around to my behind. He forces me close to him and I continue rubbing him.

He moans again.

I pump his heavy member harder and he clenches.

I pump harder.

He explodes over the floor.

I feel the tension disappear from his body and he breathes heavily while he collapses back on the armchair.

He winks at me, smirking.

"You can dressed now," he whispers, "Thankyou."

I quickly get dressed and leave his office with a smile stretched across my face.

Romance: The Billionaire Boss

Chapter 2

I service Joel three times over the next two weeks.

Each time is more exciting than last. I can now tell when he is going to ask me to 'help' him out. When he becomes very excited and gets a charming look in his eyes, I know what he is going to ask.

But today seems different. He has the look but he seems a little distracted as he asks me into his office.

"Working hard today?" he asks flippantly.

"Yes, Joel."

"Did you edit that report like I asked?"

"It's on your desk."

"Good. Thanks," he seems to be stalling.

We stand in awkward silence for more than a few moments.

"I'll get to the point - do you have a boyfriend?"

"Um... no, not at the moment," I respond.

"Do you believe in love?"

"Love?"

"Yes. Love. Do you believe in love?"

"I believe in love."

"I have never believed in love. I've always thought that love was interchangeable with lust. I always thought the feeling of lust was mixed with feeling of love…"

"But?"

"But now, I'm not so sure. You have confused me."

"And what have I confused you about?"

"Love… or lust. I don't know. I don't understand the difference."

"Lust means that we want to shag. Love means you'll stay after we shag. That's what my best friend always says."

"Seems fair enough. If we shagged, would you stay?"

"I wouldn't be going anywhere."

I stand next to the desk in his office and he sways across to me.

He leans in and kisses me again. This kiss is different. There is real feeling behind this kiss. His lips are so tender. So delicate.

I feel like a piece of meat that is about to be used for Joel's servicing pleasure.

And I like it.

He lips tenderly kiss my neck, his strong hand pulling my hair to the side.

He kisses my shoulder and it sends shivers through me. I kiss back at his neck in the passion.

Oh, he smells so good.

As I rub my hands over his body, I become primal. This man's body is a piece of artwork. I want it. I just don't want to 'service' him, I want all of him.

I tear the jacket off his back and throw it on the floor. My hands rub all over his toned and muscular body, pushing against his strength. My hands smooth up his toned arms and around his shoulders.

Oh yes.

He takes control.

He pulls off my dress and my underwear in one clean movement, and continues to undress himself. As his pants go down, so do I. I yank down his jocks and expose a smooth and waxed manhood. Oh yes.

He is big. And solid. Yum.

I put him in my mouth and bounce my head up and down his shaft. He moans. The faster I bounce my head, the louder he moans. Yes – Joel is shouting for more. I love it.

He pulls me up by the shoulders and lays me across the desk. I am so wet, I want him inside me. I frantically push the piles of papers aside on his office desk to give myself some room.

He guides his member towards my pussy, and slides in. Oh yes – I have the world's best looking man inside me. Oh yes.

I feel him deep inside me, he is stretching at the width of my lips, and he begins to thrust. I rub my hands up and down his arms – I want to eat him all up.

Amazing.

He thrusts at me harder, pumping his member into me.

He brings my legs up to his shoulders and as his hips thrust into me, his arms pull my legs back down. Oh yes.

He jams me and I try to grip the table's edge to hold still. His member is reaching me in places that haven't been touched before. I become hot, and I start to shake.

Wow.

I run my hands up to his manly chest and it is everything I ever imagined. It is so toned and hot. So strong.

He withdraws and aggressively turns my body over, leaning me forward over the table. I poke my wet pussy out for him and he quickly finds the spot. Oh yes, he finds the spot.

Wow.

He continues to pump and I quickly orgasm. I hold onto the table and he jams me one last time.

Wow.

When he withdraws he slumps back to his favourite armchair. I roll over on the table and stare at the roof.

Oh yes. What a moment.

It takes a while for my breathing to come back to normal.

"I have never had sex with a personal assistant before," he breaks the long silence.

"Was it just sex?" I ask.

He doesn't respond.

He knows that it was more than 'just sex.' I could feel that between the two of us.

"I need a toy," Joel states strongly.

"What sort of toy?" I ask.

"One I can use all the time. Whenever I want."

"Yes but… what sort of toy are we talking about?" I try to clarify his request.

"You."

Romance: The Billionaire Boss

Chapter 3

It has now been five weeks since I started this give and take role. I have experienced a lot. I also have a new diamond necklace and a new car. But I'm not sure how I feel about that.

After our moment in the office, things have escalated quickly. It's turned from 'just sex' into a little more thrilling.

I have now become his toy. To use whenever he wants.

One day, we will passionately make love in his office and the next he'll whip me like a little whore. I can tell that he is really confused about what he wants from our relationship. He seems to float between love and lust.

I don't mind. I love the adventure. If you were to ask me if I would like to settle down with Joel, I would say yes – of course I would say yes.

But this role of personal assistant is thrilling. I love this adventure. I never know what is going to happen next. And I certainly didn't see this coming.

He gave me very strict instructions when I walked in the door this morning, and here I am. Things really have been taken to the next level.

I am going to be used as his plaything. All day.

Ouch.

That one hurts.

But I like it.

I hear Joel's hand raise again and he lands it with a spank on my behind. The clap leaves me red, sore and stinging.

Oh yes - I love it.

"Excuse me," he whispers in my ear.

I try to move my head to bite his ear in passion but he has tied me tight this time. I am naked and face down on the soft rug in his office, my arms and legs stretching out like a star over the floor.

The ropes are tied to the tables at each end of the office. If I pulled hard enough at them, I could escape… but I don't want to. As Joel leaves the office, I am left vulnerable. My behind stings with redness but my head lies down and I wait for him to return.

If anyone walked through his office doors, they would see my naked body face down on the floor and my behind a glowing red. I am very vulnerable.

Naked, tied up and alone in the office of a billionaire.

Joel loves to use me as his toy. He wanders in and out throughout the afternoon, in between meetings, and spanks me, plays with me and passionately makes love to me. I wait for the moment when he takes off his dashing suit. That means he is willing to end his day.

I want that moment.

I have around 30 mins to rest on the floor between plays. That's how long he usually has a meeting for. It will probably take my behind that long to recover from the latest spanking.

The sunshine has started to fade in office when he wanders back in. It must be mid-afternoon, still too early for the love making. I love the anticipation of not knowing what's coming next.

This time, I hear his footsteps circle my behind. He wanders down one side of my body and stops. I try to look behind and catch a glimpse of his body standing over me. I love the fact that I am his muse. I love the way he adores my body.

He moans with pleasure as he runs his fingers up my behind and up my back. I listen to him take off his jacket, unclip his cuffs and roll up his sleeve. His strong, large hands gently touch my behind and rub my curves. I am going to love this.

I feel his hands caress my butt and wander down my crack until they reach my passion. I squirm as his fingers dance around my pussy. He feels so strong against my wetness.

When his fingers enter me, I squeal with passion.

"Shhh...." he whispers in my ear, "Or I might have to spank you again."

I can tell he is smiling as he talks.

He rubs his fingers inside me, forcing me to bite my bottom lip in an attempt to stay quiet. I pull hard at the ropes, but not too hard.

"How many fingers have I got in?" he whispers.

"Three?"

Spank.

"Wrong."

Ouch.

"One?" I guess again.

Spank.

"Two?"

"Correct."

He rubs my tender behind with one hand and caresses the inside of my pussy with his other. Oh yes, that feels good. His dominance over me is clear.

Cold liquid leaks over my anal and I feel a strong finger pushing in.

Oh.

His finger forces into my anal and I clench.

"Relax," he whispers again.

"I've never had it there before."

"Relax..."

He pushes it in until my buttock muscles relax. Once I relax my muscles, he squeezes another finger in. He can tell it hurts but I can tell he loves it. He begins to jam his fingers into and out of my anal with rhythm. I moan with delight, but as soon as I do, he stops.

His footsteps move around to the front of my tied up body and I suddenly find his groin in front of my face. Unzipping his fly, he pulls out his strong member and guides it towards my mouth. It smells like man.

His hand holds my chin up and I wrap my lips around his member. It tastes like man. Real man. It is strong, hard, and I want it. I want it all. I lash his member with my tongue and salvia until he pulls away.

His fly zips up.

Grrrrr.... He has left me hanging again. I want his cock. I need his cock. He shouldn't leave. He should take me now. I want his cock inside me.

But I know he won't.

I hear the office door close again and he leaves me lying there, on the floor like his dirty piece of meat. My head hits the ground as I sigh. I can't wait until he takes me again.

Luckily, I don't have to wait long. I have only been waiting for around half an hour until he enters the room again. He fiddles around at his desk for a period of time, not even acknowledging the presence of a naked woman tied face down to the floor of his office. I lie in waiting as he attends to his work matters.

He even takes a phone call at his desk. He talks work while I lie completely naked waiting for him. The anticipation is making me wet. I want him.

When he stops his work and starts to undress, I know it's final.

He doesn't say anything but I point by bum in the air, exposing my pussy, letting him know I am ready. I hear his clothes drop to the floor and his shoes slide off. Again, I feel a cold liquid drip over my pussy, not that I need it.

His hands pull my butt cheeks apart and then he wrestles with them with his strength. He forces my hips into the ground before his thick, hard cock forces its way in and pulls on the sides of my lips. He pushes it very deep inside me and holds it there. His hands run over my back, and I feel his eyes adoring my womanly curves. His strong touch drives shivers through me. He begins to grip the flesh of my behind, gripping it tightly. He squeezes the flesh hard. Very hard.

Slap.

He spanks my behind with passion.

I can tell he is going to be aggressive, he seems almost angry. That last meeting must have been a bad one.

But a good one for me.

Spank.

Oh yes.

He starts.

He pounds me with all that pent up aggression and he is quick, like a jack-hammer. Striking and striking. Smashing his cock in and out. Slamming me into the rug.

Yes.

His hands pull my arse cheeks apart and I point my bum further in the air.

Yes.

His body weight is coming down on-top of me, his dominance is clear.

Spank.

He groans with primal aggression.

Oh yes.

He is so strong. So aggressive.

After a few short minutes, he stops. He becomes slower, more deliberate. He tenderly reaches across, feeling my breasts and tweaking with my nipples. I like that. It feels good to have his cock stay inside me. His passion is clear.

His hands run all over my body until he comes closer to my butt. His fingers feel their way around. He pushes it in back in.

Yes.

My butt is tight but I like having both holes filled. He fingers my behind while his manhood keeps caressing my pussy, gently in and out with rhythm. The rush of orgasm suddenly comes over me.

Oh yes!

I feel hot and I start to shake.

Yes!

He stops.

He withdraws.

He is in control here.

Damn.

His footsteps circle around my body until they come to my face.

He kneels down and I grab his hard member with my mouth. It is so long and solid. Standing upright. He reaches over me and begins to finger my pussy again. Oh, that feels good.

I'm coming again.

The harder I pump his cock with my mouth, the harder he jams me with his fingers. I squeal as I come again.

He takes over on his member and he pumps it only the way a man can. His juice squirts on my face.

Oh yes sir!

We both take a few moments to catch our breath.

He stands, kisses me on the cheek, and begins to untie me.

As he unties me, he says, "Tomorrow, can you organise an eleven o'clock meeting between me and the new buyers?"

"Yes," I agree.

He smiles again and kisses me on the lips.

I love being his dirty little personal assistant.

Romance: The Billionaire Boss

Chapter 4

When I arrive at work the next morning, Joel is waiting in his office for me. I am still sore from yesterday so I'm not sure if I'll be able to take much today.

"Good morning," I say cheerily.

He doesn't respond.

"Your first meeting this morning is at 9.30 with the buyers from Davis and Co. and then we have the eleven o'clock with the new buyers," I state, remembering his diary.

Again, he does not respond.

Instead he stands looking out of the window in office, his hands folded behind his back.

"Everything ok?"

"No," he finally responds.

"Ok. What's wrong?"

"You can't work here anymore."

"Sorry?"

"You can't work here anymore."

"Why not?"

"Because."

"That's not good enough. I'm good at this job."

"And that's the problem."

"That I'm good at the job?"

"Yes."

"Why is that a problem?"

"Because no-one that has come before you has been good at the job. No-one has been so…" he doesn't finish the sentence. Instead, he turns and looks at his desk, "If you could please pack your things and be out in an hour."

"You can't just sack me. What about all the moments we spent together?"

He shrugs his shoulders.

"There was chemistry there, Joel. You can't deny that. Tell me that you didn't feel that chemistry?"

He doesn't respond and still doesn't look at me.

"What's wrong?" I demand.

Without looking at me, he offers an explanation, "I need a personal assistant. Not a lover. And you are neither. You distract me from the business of making money. I can't have that. I can't be distracted. Your job role is for someone to help me run this business. Profits have fallen over the last six weeks. Clearly, this is not working and I am not thinking straight. I can't have you in my life."

"So you're going to choose money over what we have?"

"And what do we have?"

I am shattered, "I shouldn't have to spell that out for you. You could feel it. Don't lie to me and tell me that you couldn't feel the passion between us. What we have is real."

"We have nothing but our working relationship. Don't pretend that you are something that you are not, don't think that I can't live without you. You only come to work into this office because I pay you. And I pay you well. I only pay you for your looks. Nothing more. You're an assistant to the boss. That's it. What we have is the principal of give and take. That's the principle of life."

"That's not true. Your precious principle of give and take is flawed. It doesn't explain what we have. With what we have – we both give. There is no take. We have something more than you've ever experienced before."

"Don't fool yourself, Amy. You're replaceable. And your replacement starts in one hour. I want you out of this office by then."

"That's it? It's over?"

"Don't worry, I'll look after you financially. I'll make sure you're ok."

"I don't want your money."

He doesn't answer, and still there is no eye contact.

"Look at me," I demand.

He doesn't look. He clearly does not want eye contact.

"Look at me."

Again, he doesn't look.

I can feel the tears starting to well up inside me. I can't cry in-front of him, I won't let him have that pleasure. In a heat of passion, I turn and run from his office.

After an elevator ride where I hide my tears, I walk towards the building exit, but Melissa is just walking in. She sees the look on my face.

"Oh dear," she says. She knows.

"Come on," she continues, "Sit down over here."

Melissa places a consoling arm around me and leads me to the couch at the foyer of the building. I sit and try to compose myself, wiping the tears away with a tissue.

"You got too close, didn't you?"

I shrug my shoulders.

"It's not your fault dear, it's your personality and looks. They have sucked him in. He wouldn't have been able to resist you."

"It's not fair."

"No, dear, it's not."

"I like him. No, I just don't like him - I think I'm in love with him. It's more than anything I have ever experienced before. I don't want his money, or wealth. I don't even like the new car that he bought me. It's a stupid car. I just like him."

Melissa nods.

"I can't let him go. I have to go back up there and talk some sense into him. I have never felt like this before and I can tell that he hasn't either. What we have is special. I can't just throw that away."

"You can't go back up there, dear."

"I have to. I can't let him go."

"If you go back up there, he'll only push you further away."

"What am I supposed to do then?"

"You'll have to wait until he comes to you. If what you said is real, then he will realize that he misses it very quickly. He'll come back to you. You have to wait for him to come back to you."

"What if he doesn't? What if he doesn't understand what he is feeling?"

"I think he will."

"What makes you so sure?"

"Because I'm going to have a word to him," Melissa leaves me on the couch, and storms off to the elevator with a determined pace. Alone, I leave the building and hail the nearest taxi to escape to the comfort of my bed.

I am shattered.

He used me.

He used me as one of his women to service his pleasures. I was nothing more than that. I am just another one of his long line of women. I was just a piece of meat to him.

After the time we spent together, how could he use me like that? How could he reject the moments of passion that we spent together. I felt it and I'm sure that he felt it. His kisses were full of passion, lust and desire. It wasn't just sex. That was something more.

No, don't kid yourself, Amy.

I am just a piece of meat that was used for his servicing pleasure.

As I feel the tears starting to run down my face, I tuck my head into my pillow and cry some more. The pillow is already wet from the hours of crying that I have done since I left the office.

How could I have been so silly?

How could I have become one of his targets?

He promised me that I wasn't just another girl!

The tears don't stop. They keep rolling.

He rejected everything that I thought was real. Was it real? Of course it was real. I felt it. And he felt it too. But he is too confused about life to realize.

The principle of give and take?! What sort of life philosophy is that? It doesn't make sense. It doesn't explain love.

I am shattered.

He has taken me for a ride. I am just another one of his many girls. After our many moments of passion, he has dropped me like a ball.

Ouch.

When I eventually climb back out of bed, I head straight to the fridge to devour the remaining ice-cream. Sitting on the couch in my apartment with the curtains drawn, stopping any daylight creeping in, I watch an old romantic comedy movie to distract myself.

I cry when the movie wants me to cry and I laugh when the movie wants me to laugh. Before I know it, the tub of ice-cream is finished and a pile of wet tissues sit next to my couch.

After the third romantic comedy movie in a row, there is a knock at the door.

I pretend not to hear it.

I am not answering the door for anyone today.

But they are persistent.

The knock becomes louder and louder.

I finally climb off the couch, wipe my eyes, and go to answer the door.

As I open the door, I am shocked.

There is a tall, dark figure waiting on my steps.

It is Joel.

Joel Hill.

What does he want? Round two with another one of his many girls?

"Hello."

His voice is as seductive as always.

I don't respond.

"Hi," he continues.

I am not amused.

"This morning…"

"Don't," I interrupt him, "I don't want to be another one of your girls."

"You're not. I mean, you are. I mean, you're not just one of the girls," he is stumbling over his words.

That is unusual for someone so confident.

"I'm sorry," he states.

I don't respond.

"I'm confused."

"You're confused? What about me?"

"I'm sorry," he states again and then pauses, "May I come in?"

I hesitate – I don't want to let him in but my politeness gets the better of me. I let him into the lounge room.

Quickly, I realize that dark room is covered in tissues from my tears and hide them away, along with the empty ice-cream tub.

"Been a good afternoon?" he asks. Obviously, my best attempts to hide the evidence have not worked.

"It's been an afternoon."

"I'm sorry, Amy. I don't know what came over me this morning. I had a meeting with some investors last night and they were really concerned with the drop in profits. The amount of profits that we've dropped over the last few weeks is not sustainable."

"So, I'm to blame for the drop in profits?"

"No," his beautiful eyes look straight at me, "I'm to blame. It's my fault that the profits dropped."

"The why sack me?"

"Because you're too beautiful."

"Too beautiful? That's not a reason to sack anyone. Too beautiful is the dumbest thing I have ever heard."

"You are too beautiful. I can't stop thinking about you. I think about you all the time. I think about you in meetings, at breakfast, at presentations and all night long. I haven't been able to sleep for weeks because I keep running over and over in my head what I'm going to say to you each morning."

"You never talk to me in the mornings?"

"Exactly. I have these great, witty, scripted lines that I want to say to you each morning but I can never get them out. I want to come arrive in the morning and tell you how beautiful you look or how great you smell, but I never can. I want to tell you that you fill my dreams night after night but I can't. I can never say it. I'm always too nervous."

"Nervous? You don't seem like the nervous type Joel."

"I'm not. But you make me nervous. I have never felt like this before."

"Why did you come here, Joel?"

"I wasn't going to come. I was going to let you go. But then my aunty stormed into my office today and demanded that I make the right choice."

"Your aunty?"

"Melissa Hill. She works in accounts."

"Melissa is your aunty?"

"Yes. I told her that I could buy her whatever she wanted in life, and that she doesn't need to work, but she likes to work. She wouldn't give up the job, it's her life. And she's good with accounts, very trustworthy."

He smiles at me with his stunning eyes.

Damn.

No.

Don't be taken in by him. Don't be one of his many conquests. But I can't resist. He has gotten me. I am smitten.

"So, what now?" I ask.

He shrugs his shoulders, "Do you feel the same?"

I am shocked he even asked. How could he not feel it?

"Of course. You are everything that I ever imagined. I want you to be a part of my life every single day. I want to wake up next to you and make you breakfast. I want you to be the person that gives me a shoulder massage when I'm too stressed. I want you make you happy and I want you to make me happy. That's how I feel."

He smiles and starts to walk towards me.

"Wait," I stop him, "What about the business? What about your precious profits?"

"I've already sold the business."

"What? You can't sell a billion dollar business in a matter of hours."

"I can and I have. A group have been chasing me for a number of years, trying to get me to sell. I called them up today and sold. We have to work out the finer details, but in principle, the company is gone. I came right over after I closed the deal. There is no-one else that I would rather celebrate with."

"Really? What if I had said no?"

"If you had said no to me? I don't think I would have taken no for an answer."

He moves around the side of my body and whispers in my ear, "You and me. No more give and take. Just us and where-ever we want to go."

"No more give and take?"

"No more dumb philosophies."

His soft tone sends shivers through my body.

It is too hard.

I can't resist looks like that.

Damn it. I can't say no.

I want to say no. I want to tell him how much he has hurt me today. But I can't resist him. I have wanted to be more than just a personal assistant since we first meet.

He kisses my shoulder and it sends shivers through me. I kiss back at his neck.

Oh, he smells so good. Perfect.

As I rub my hands over his body, I become primal. I know where I am and I know what I want. This man's body is a piece of artwork. I can't ignore it any more.

I grab his hand and lead him into my bedroom. I tear the jacket off his back and throw it on the floor. My hands rub all over his toned and muscular body as he kisses me in passion. My hands smooth up his toned arms and around his shoulders.

Oh yes.

He takes control.

He pulls off my dress and my underwear in one clean movement, and continues to undress himself. As his pants go down, so do I. I yank down his jocks and expose a smooth and waxed manhood. Oh yes.

He is big. And solid. Yum.

I put him in my mouth and bounce my head up and down his shaft. He moans. The faster I bounce my head, the louder he moans. Yes – Joel is shouting for more. I love it.

He pulls me up by the shoulders and lays me across the bed. I am so wet, I want his hardness inside me. He obliges and guides his member towards my pussy, sliding into my pussy. Oh yes – I have the world's best looking man inside me. Oh yes.

I feel him deep inside me, he is stretching at the width of my lips, and he begins to thrust. I rub my hands up and down his arms – I want to eat him all up.

He is amazing.

He thrusts me more, pumping his member into me.

He brings my legs up to his shoulders and as his hips thrust into me, his arms pull my legs back down. Oh yes.

He jams me and I try to grip the bed's edge to hold still. His member is reaching me in places that haven't been touched before. I become hot, and I start to shake.

Wow.

I run my hands up to his manly chest and it is everything I ever imagined. It is so toned and hot. So strong.

He withdraws and aggressively turns my body over, leaning me forward over the bed. I poke my wet pussy out for him and he quickly finds the spot. Oh yes, he finds the spot.

Wow.

He continues to pump and I quickly orgasm. I hold onto the table and he jams me one last time.

Wow.

When he withdraws he slumps to the bed. I roll over and stare at the roof.

Oh yes. What a moment.

"I love you more than anything in the world," he states in a moment of post-sex bliss, "Move in with me."

"No," I state, "Let's get out of here. Let's disappear from this side of the world. Let's get away from all this craziness."

"I would love to. Where to?"

"I don't care. Let's forget about it all and just be us."

He smiles, "I don't care either. As long as we're together…"

Romance: Interviewing the Billionaire

Jodi Cooper

Copyright © 2014

Published by Run Free Publishing

All rights reserved.

No part of this publication may be reproduced, stored in a retrieval system, or transmitted, in any form or by any means without the prior permission in writing of the publisher.

Romance: Interviewing the Billionaire

Chapter 1

I am so nervous.

I have never been comfortable in stilettoes.

My stomach is filled with butterflies and my hand is shaking as I hold onto the champagne glass.

The richest people in the country are all sitting around me in this ball room. Most of them are old men with well-fitted suits who want to talk about how they made their millions. They laugh at their own in-jokes about how rich they are. I smile politely to their arrogance.

But they are not why I am here.

I am here for Sam Symonds.

Sam Symonds – the man who founded an internet search engine but now spends his days campaigning for donations to make the world a better place. He made his money early on in the dot-com business and then he sold up big to another company. He made a lot of money out of the sale.

I watch as Sam Symonds walks to the podium to deliver his speech. He doesn't look like your usual computer nerd. He is distinguished, tall, broad shouldered, and has a glow of health radiating off him. His eyes are crystal clear and his skin looks so soft that all I want to do is kiss it.

His looks made him the poster boy for internet success and he used that exposure to raise funds for those less well off.

He also used that exposure for a playboy lifestyle full of women – but I hope that lifestyle is in the past.

This gala ball is for raising funds for starving children in Africa. A very worthy cause.

I scored an invite through the large fashion/current affairs magazine that I work for because I am writing a piece about Sam. Although he has had a lot of exposure, not a lot has been written about the Sam the person. That's the one thing I want to write about. I want to write about what makes him so motivated. I want to give the readers something that they did not know about Sam Symonds.

Sam's keynote speech is amazing. I hang off his every word. His hands illustrate a story and he has the whole audience captivated. He could lead people to where-ever he wants to take them. I'm glad he chooses to lead them to a worthy place.

I sit back down to the large table with a movie heart-throb, the CFO of a major bank, and a character whose face looks like a cartoon. The champagne glass shakes in my hand as I raise a toast to the conclusion of the last speech.

Everyone is very polite to me – not friendly but polite. They talk small chat but they don't really engage in conversation. They know I have to power to paint their public picture however I want, so they entertain me. It may be cynical but the ones who are the nicest are the ones who have a press releases coming out shortly.

I am introduced to numerous men and women, so many faces that I have seen before. I shake so my hands that my wrist is almost sore.

If I was a teenage girl, I would be screaming the ears off this place with excitement. I try to control myself. I act classy. Sophisticated.

That is until I am introduced to Sam Symonds.

Wow.

He is as gorgeous as the pictures make out.

He is so perfect in every way - broad shoulders, perfect cheekbones, handsome and dashing.

He walks straight up to me,

"Hi, I'm Sam."

He holds out his large hand to shake as an introduction.

I freeze.

I don't move a muscle.

The world's most beautiful man is in-front of me and I cannot say a word.

After a few moments of awkward silence, he takes away his hand, provides me with a nice smile and moves onto the next conversation.

I am still frozen.

How embarrassing...

When I arrive at work the next morning, all the girls of the office ask about my night. I provide them with a whimsical explanation of the night, obviously glossing over the moment of frozen embarrassment.

They are hooked on my every word, engrossed in the tales of meeting the world's richest people. They stare at me with their wide-eyed excitement, envious of my night.

"And Sam Symonds?"

The room goes silent.

I shake my head,

"Unfortunately, I didn't get to talk to him."

Which was true. I didn't talk to him, although I wanted too.

But after I make the statement, there is an awkward silence across the room.

"What?" I question.

"You haven't been to your desk yet, have you?" one of the girls state.

"I haven't made it that far this morning, no. Why?"

Smiles drift across the faces of the girls gathered in the lunch room, as they slowly start to make their way to my desk.

I leave the lunch room with interpretation, wondering what is waiting at my desk.

When I round the corner in the office, I notice a large bunch of flowers on my desk. This alone is a big enough shock but it is the card that really shocks me.

It reads

'Sorry we couldn't chat the last night but I would like to take you to dinner. Meet you at 'Stanza's Restaurant' at 8.'

Signed 'Sam Symonds'.

Romance: Interviewing the Billionaire

Chapter 2

I arrive at the small Italian restaurant and ask for Sam. The waiter looks me up and down, and then guides me to where Sam is waiting at a private table out the back of the restaurant.

"This is my private room," he states in his manly voice as the waiter sits me down, "You'll find that most famous people have their own private room at their regular restaurants."

"And what is the purpose of this private room?" I stumble over my words.

"It is for when we don't want people to know what we're doing. If I wanted the paparazzi to photograph us, I would have sat in the front room of the restaurant, next to the window. But when you want a private dinner, you ask for the private room. It's so the world doesn't know everything that we do."

"But you are trying to raise funds. Don't you want to be seen everywhere?"

"Everyone needs some time off."

I am so impressed. He is intelligent, a great conversationalist, and I become increasingly lost in his dashing eyes as the night wears on.

I left work early to prepare for dinner. I don't often get invited out to dinner – let alone dinner with the world's most beautiful man. I certainly didn't have to spend a lot of time choosing what to wear. I really hope he doesn't notice that I am wearing the same dress as last night.

After a few drinks of wine, I start to loosen up and am able to get my words out.

He laughs at my very bad stories and seems genuinely interested in me. He is either a very good actor or this is the greatest moment of my life.

"I do have to ask though Sam…"

"Yes?"

"Why dinner?"

"Because I like to eat at this time of night."

"No, why dinner with me? Most of the people at the fundraiser dinner just wanted to be nice, but you – you've taken it a little further."

He pauses and sighs.

I wait for his response.

"You know when you meet someone, your instincts instantly tell whether you like a person?"

"Yes," I nod.

"Well, when I saw your eyes, I knew that I liked you. I knew that I had to talk to you. And when you didn't talk, I couldn't let it go."

I am shocked into saying nothing again.

"And when I walked up to you, I realised how beautiful you are."

I am not sure that I will ever be able to talk again. Sam Symonds, the world's most dashing man, has just called me beautiful.

"Beautiful?" I am shocked.

"Yes, very beautiful. I've thought about you all day. I just had to get to know you."

"You know that I am writing an article about you, don't you?" my scepticism gets the better of me.

He nods.

"So dinner isn't an attempt to influence that article?"

"No," he shakes his head, "If I was going to do that, I would try and influence your editor. They would be the one I would go after."

"So, dinner is just dinner then?"

"I hope it's more than dinner."

"More?"

He smiles cheekily, "Hopefully."

"You could pick any girl you want. Why pick the one that is writing an article about you?"

What I am doing?!

This should be the most dazzling moment of my dating life, and all I am doing is questioning why he has invited me here.

Sam shrugs his shoulders, "When you're at the top, it's quite a lonely game. People only want to meet you superficially. And when you try to get to know people, they doubt why you would want to get to know them."

Damn. That's exactly what I have just done. Quickly, I have to change the conversation. I'll talk about the last article I just wrote for the magazine,

"Did you know that the average male doubts his penis size is average?"

What!

What I am saying?!

Sam looks as shocked as me. The combination of nerves and wine does not make me a great conversationalist.

"Do they? Um...."

Sam doesn't know what to say. Quick, I have to say something else...

"Yes. And as a girl you're always told never to tell a man the truth about his size."

"Never?"

"Why... you're supposed to lie if it's not average."

"Really? So all those girls were lying to me," he smiles.

"Could have been," I wink.

I'm stunned. What have I just said!

Mental note to future self – never drink three glasses of wine when trying to make conversation with the world's most beautiful man.

"Um..." Sam doesn't know what to say.

"They also say that most men are either show-ers or growers."

What! I should really stop talking.

"Show-ers or growers?"

"Yes. They either show their size right away or they grow into it."

"Wow. There you go. I've learnt something new today," at least Sam is still smiling, "You seem to know a lot about the subject?"

"I had to write an article about for the magazine. You know, one of those articles that you don't want to write but you have to."

"Ahh yes. That explains it then. What else have you written about?"

"Apart from penis sizes, I have written about designer vaginas, breast implants gone wrong, sex clubs…" I joke.

"And now you're doing an article about me? Should I be worried?" he laughs.

"But I've also written about past presidents, political landscapes, foreign trade and travel."

Yes! I have regained some dignity.

Luckily, the conversation with Sam only goes up from there. We talk about life in general for both of us and I am surprised to hear how normal is life is. I always imagined that his life would be one crazy collection of wild parties but the things he talks about are remarkably mundane.

There is an air of discontentment when he talks about his rich and famous lifestyle.

"I want to escape from it. I just haven't had a reason to yet," he states.

I don't want this night to end. He is such a great conversationalist. We talk until there is no-one left in the restaurant, and we get the nod from the waiter that it is closing time.

Unfortunately, the night has come to an end. After we leave the restaurant and Sam hails a cab down for me, his hand reaches across to touch my hand.

Oh.

Wow.

My heart rate screams faster. I think it is about to burst out of my chest, it is beating that hard.

Sam leans down and kisses me gently on the cheek.

Wow.

His lips are tender and soft, everything that I imagined them to be.

Oh wow.

Sam smiles his cheeky smile as I climb into the cab in a daze.

Romance: Interviewing the Billionaire

Chapter 3

Over the next few days, I float on cloud nine. I can't believe this has happened to me. This is everything that I had dreamed of. I go through my usual daily routine with a buzz of excitement and I walk with a spring in my step. My mind is lost in a cloud of passion, reliving my moments with Sam over and over.

I want to tell the world.

I want to call up everyone I know and tell them.

But I can't.

I can't tell anyone. I have to keep my relationship with Sam a secret.

I don't tell the girls at the office. I don't tell my girlfriends. I don't even tell my best friend. They probably won't believe me anyway.

As the days go past, I can't stop thinking about it. The greatest moment of my life and I can't share it with anyone…

But then I see it.

Just when I started to believe that Sam Symonds was genuine, I see something that shatters my belief.

A news story that drives into my heart like a stake. I am breathless.

The news story is of Sam Symonds, surrounded by a group of hot bikini clad women, dancing around the pool like it's a sex party.

Then I read the headline.

It reads 'Sam does it again! More women than he can handle in one wild night!'

I am shattered.

He used me.

He used me as one of his women to give him a report in the magazine. I am just another one of his women.

After the night we spent together, how could he use me like that?

I am just a piece of meat for his servicing pleasure.

When I feel the tears starting to run down my face, I run to the nearest bathroom and cry into my hands.

How could I have been so stupid?

How could I have become one of his prey?

He promised me that I wasn't just another girl!

The tears don't stop. They keep rolling.

There were three bikini clad women on that news story – all lounging over my Sam.

My Sam.

I am shattered.

He has taken me for a ride. I am just another one of his many girls. After our night of passion, this is what I'm presented with.

Ouch.

I make up an excuse about my health and take the rest of the day off to fall into my bed and cry.

The tubs of ice-cream pile up next to my bed as I cuddle my pillow and I sob for hours. After many daylight hours in bed, my doorbell rings.

No. I don't want to answer the door. Go away.

I am not responding to any requests for contact today.

They ring the doorbell again. And again. They are persistent.

I finally climb out of bed, wipe my eyes, and go to answer the door.

My shock is obvious as I answer the door.

There is a tall, dark figure waiting on my steps.

It is Sam.

Sam Symonds.

"Hello."

His voice is as seductive as always.

I don't respond.

"Much like our first meeting…" he continues.

I am not amused.

"That magazine cover…"

"Don't," I interrupt him, "I don't want to be another one of your many girls. And I don't look very good in a bikini."

"I don't want to see you in a bikini."

Ouch.

"I mean, I do," he tries to dig himself out of the hole he has just dug for himself, "But I mean, not in that way. Well, in that way but not in that way," he is stumbling over his words.

This is the first time I have seen him look vulnerable.

"I'm sorry," he states.

I don't respond.

"The story is old."

"What?"

"The story. It's an old picture. The film clip is over three years old."

"How dare you. How dare you come here and make up excuses."

The anger wells up inside me to make tears in my eyes.

I don't want to cry. I don't want to let him know how much he has hurt me.

"The photos are over three years old. Look at the photo. Do I have a tattoo on my chest?"

He holds out a news clip photo as evidence.

He is right – the tattoo is missing from the photo.

"I've had that tattoo for three years."

"I don't understand."

"My people released that story."

"Your people? Why would they do that?"

"They want to sell more tickets to the next fundraiser. If we're going to get people to the fundraisers, then I have to be on the headlines."

"Your own people did this?"

He nods, "Being famous is not a nice place to be."

He smiles at me with his stunning eyes.

Damn.

No.

Don't be taken in by him.

Don't be another one of his many conquests.

"I will leave the rich and famous for you. You have given me a reason to let it all go. I will go anywhere in the world that you want to go. Let's escape together."

He moves around the side of my body and whispers in my ear, "Anywhere in the world."

His soft tone sends shivers through my body.

It is too hard.

I can't resist looks like that.

Damn it. I can't say no.

I have always wanted him. I have dreamt about this so often. Whenever I saw him talk on television, I always thought he was talking to me. I always wanted to be his love interest.

He kisses my shoulder and it sends shivers through me. I kiss back at his neck.

Oh, he smells so good. He smells like I always dreamed he would smell. Perfect.

As I rub my hands over his body, I become primal. I know where I am and I know what I want. This man's body is a piece of artwork. I can't ignore it any more.

I grab his hand and lead him into my apartment. I tear the jacket off his back and throw it on the floor. My hands rub all over his toned and muscular body. My hands smooth up his toned arms and around his shoulders.

Oh yes.

He takes control.

He pulls off my dress and my underwear in one clean movement, and continues to undress himself. As his pants go down, so do I. I yank down his jocks and expose a smooth and waxed manhood. Oh yes.

He is big. And solid.

I put his manhood in my mouth and bounce my head up and down his shaft. He moans. The faster I bounce my head, the louder he moans. Yes – Sam Symonds is shouting for more. I love it.

He pulls me up by the shoulders and lays me across the bed. I am so wet, I want his hardness inside me. He obliges and guides his member towards my pussy, sliding into me. Oh yes – I have the world's best looking man inside me. Oh yes.

I feel him deep inside me, he is stretching at the width of my lips, and he begins to thrust. I rub my hands up and down his arms – I want to eat him all up.

He is amazing.

He thrusts me more, pumping his member into me.

He brings my legs up to his shoulders and as his hips thrust into me, his arms pull my legs back down. Oh yes.

He jams me and I try to grip the bed's edge to hold still. His member is reaching me in places that haven't been touched before. I become hot, and I start to shake.

Wow. I run my hands up to his manly chest and it is everything I ever imagined. It is so toned and hot. So strong.

He withdraws and aggressively turns my body over, leaning me forward over the bed. I poke my wetness out for him and he quickly finds the spot. Oh yes, he finds the spot.

Wow.

He continues to pump and I quickly orgasm. I hold onto the bed and he jams me one last time.

Wow.

When he withdraws he slumps to the bed. I roll over and stare at the roof.

Oh yes. What a moment…

"I'm sorry," he whispers in a moment of post-sex bliss.

"Let's get out of here, Sam. Let's disappear. Let's get away from all this craziness."

"Where to?"

"Italy. I've always wanted to live in Italy. Let's forget about it all and just be us."

He smiles.

"Goodbye lifestyle. Hello Italy…"

Romance: The Billionaire Actor

Jodi Cooper

Copyright © 2014

Published by Run Free Publishing

All rights reserved.

No part of this publication may be reproduced, stored in a retrieval system, or transmitted, in any form or by any means without the prior permission in writing of the publisher.

Romance: The Billionaire Actor

Chapter 1

Not a lot happens in our small town.

Everyday it's the same people, the same jobs and the same men to choose out of.

We get the occasional tourist caravan drifting through, searching for the story about 'Billy the Gunslinger' who shot this town apart in the days of the Wild West.

Sigh.

And then the news came through.

None of us believed it.

Hollywood was coming to town.

It seems that someone important got hold of the story of 'Billy the Gunslinger' and wanted to make a movie about him. And what better place to make that movie than where the story actually took place? We will get three days of shooting - three days where Hollywood will roll into our small town.

And just when it seemed life couldn't get any more exciting – it did.

Robert Tatum was cast in the lead role for the film.

Robert Tatum.

The same Robert Tatum that had lit up my life, night after night. The same Robert Tatum that stole my heart so many times. The same Robert Tatum that made everything else in the world disappear.

My Robert Tatum.

The richest actor in Hollywood.

A Billionaire.

And when the casting call went out for star-struck women to play a minor role in the movie, my hand went straight up. I have played a few lead roles in the theatre productions over the years but nothing like this. Nothing that was produced by Hollywood and certainly nothing that put me close to the Robert Tatum.

After months of waiting, I got the call that one of the minor roles in the film was mine. I had to be there on the first day of shooting but I got to act opposite the man I had lust after for so long…

I arrive on the day of the movie shoot so nervous.

So, so nervous.

It is good that there is a make-up trailer on-site because I haven't slept in days. The make-up staff make me feel like a movie star. They dress me in olden day clothes, do my make-up and pamper me like I haven't been pampered before.

I haven't landed a speaking role in the movie, my only role is to 'giggle and be impressed' as Billy the Gunslinger rides past on his horse. After the make-up and dressing is finished, the assistant to the Director has a word to me about the brief role I have to play.

"When you see Robert ride up on his horse for the first time, act star-struck," he says in his thick Hollywood voice, "Then as he gets closer, start to giggle."

"Don't worry," I tell him, "Acting star-struck is going to be easy."

Romance: The Billionaire Actor

Chapter 2

I wait nervously for the first shoot of the film on location. They have already shot most of the film in the studio but wanted the outside screens to be shot on location. Although it will only make up a small portion of the film, the location will add to the authenticity.

And what a job they have done to this town. They have transformed one of the dirt roads out the back of the town into the main road of a Wild West gunslinger town. They have transformed old, unused buildings into bustling saloons. They have taken empty buildings and changed them completely. Although the transformation wouldn't have even been a blimp on the movies budget, it is the biggest investment this town has seen in years.

Looking down at the street - dressed in an old, long dress - I feel like I am in the days of the old westerns. I look around as the sun is just starting to set on the horizon and dust is gently blowing around as there is no sign of modern life. In-front of me, there are no mobile phones, no televisions, and no flashing neon lights. But behind me is the biggest set-up I have ever seen - trailers upon trailers of cameras, cords and types of equipment that I have never seen before.

The sky is a beautiful combination of pink and orange, spreading across the clouds sitting quietly still in the sky.

Then I see him.

The silhouette of a strong man riding a strong horse into town. He trots gently up the road, riding like a man of upmost importance.

I am supposed to act star-stuck as 'Billy the Gunslinger' rides towards me.

But there is no acting involved.

As he comes closer, I start to make out the contours of his muscles. His shirt wraps around his strong arms and I can see his muscular chest almost begging for my hands to rub it.

His face is dirty but so wonderfully handsome. Beautiful skin, strong cheekbones and a perfect jaw – he is more handsome in real life than on big screen.

I am supposed to start to giggle as he rides closer but I can't. I am still star-struck.

"Giggle," I hear the Director shout in the background.

But I don't. My eyes connect with Robert's and we share a moment.

But it doesn't feel like a moment – it feels like forever.

He has the most dashing eyes I have ever seen. His deep blue eyes ride through me like true love.

Just as I become lost in his eyes, his horse stops.

"No," I hear the Director, "Keep riding."

But Robert doesn't.

He leaps down from his horse and lands just in-front of me. I am frozen.

In one swift moment, he embraces me. His lips land on mine and his kiss is everything I imagined. The tender soft touch of his lips contrasts against the strength of his arms, which are leaning me backwards.

His kiss drives shivers through my entire body, my head becoming lost in one moment of passionate bliss.

I am lost.

When he stops kissing me, he stands me upright, winks and then hops back on his horse to keep riding into town.

I stand, watching him in awe as he rides away.

"Cut!" the Director breaks my whimsical moment, "Brilliant. That was brilliant. Great improvisation, Robert. Great work. You really captured the playboy spirit of Billy the Gunslinger there."

I still stand in awe as Robert jumps off his horse with a smile on his face, and starts to walk towards me. But as soon as he is within a few feet of me, the Director grabs Robert and pushes him away, "Now, about the next scene we need to shoot…"

Robert tries to walk back towards me, but another assistant pushes him to the next scene as well.

Our eyes catch each other as he is being moved away.

Again, we share a moment.

But the moment is too short.

Before I know it – he is gone…

I spend the next few hours in a complete daze.

He kissed me.

He jumped off his horse and kissed me.

Robert Tatum kissed me!

He kissed me!

I can't believe it. The world seems to be spinning around me while the smile on face does not come off. People are talking to me but I don't know what they are saying. I am higher than any drug could ever get anyone.

Wow.

This is the moment of my life.

He kissed me.

And then... and then he wanted to talk to me. He must have felt it as much as me. He must have the passion, the romance, in the kiss – he must have felt the moment.

After I have undressed from the costume, I wander around the movie shoot looking for him. I have to find him. I look down every corner and over every shoulder.

"Excuse me."

The voice behind startles me.

"I've been looking for you."

I am speechless.

It is Robert.

Looking as handsome as always. His presence dwarfs me, his muscular body standing over me, his strong chest at my eye line.

I can't speak. I want to say something. I want to say profound.

Or at least say hello.

But I don't.

I can't.

Instead I just stand there like a mute.

"I enjoyed our scene today. You must be an experienced actress. You were very convincing."

I nod.

His eyebrows rise.

"Um..." I begin, "Yes. Yes. I have acted in a few plays at the local theatre."

"Oh, good. Maybe we can a coffee to chat about acting?"

"Coffee?"

"Yeah. Do you drink coffee? If you don't drink coffee, then maybe we could grab a milkshake?"

"I drink coffee."

"Oh. I haven't had a milkshake since I was a kid. A milkshake would bring back some good memories."

I laugh with the beautiful smile of Robert. He has such a cheeky smile.

"Come on, let's grab a milkshake," he laughs as he holds my hand to lead me to the catering tent. His touch sends magic through my body.

After Robert leads me hand in hand through the movie set, we round to the busy catering tent and walk straight through to a quiet spot out the back.

"This is my private room," he states in his manly voice as we sit down in our own quiet tent at the back of the catering tent, "You'll find that most famous people have their own private spot at the big movies."

"Are you enjoying the movie?" I ask.

"I love it. Billy the Gunslinger is a great person to act. He is such a player."

"Like yourself?" I say, almost in accusation.

He smiles cheekily, "Those days are behind me."

"But Billy isn't such a stretch to play?"

"Not really. I know how to be a player."

I nod.

"But I'm not anymore," he saves himself, "I guess you get to a point in your life when being a player isn't enough anymore."

"And you're at that point now?"

"I think so. I really think so. I've had enough of Hollywood. I'm done with the gossip lifestyle. I want something more. You?"

"Me?"

"Yeah, I've told you where I am at in my life. Where are you at in your life?"

"I'm bored of my little town. I want something more."

"Like Hollywood?"

"Not Hollywood. Something else. Like travel. I would love to see the world."

"I would too," his eyes smile beautifully.

"You? You would have seen the world already?"

"Not really."

"What about in 'The Mad Cross'? You would have seen the Russian mountains?"

"Filmed in a studio."

"The scene in 'Crazy Dog'? You must have travelled through the Pacific?"

He shakes his head, "Also filmed in a studio."

"What about 'The Italian Speed'?"

"Nope. All in a studio. You have seen a few movies?"

"I'm a big movie fan," I lie as I try to hide how much I have adored him in the past, "Where would you go if you could travel?"

"Maybe Amsterdam?"

"Amsterdam? I don't know a lot about Amsterdam expect that it's famous for prostitutes."

What? Why would I say that? I have used the little knowledge I have of Europe to try and impress Robert.

"Prostitutes? I'm not sure that's why I want to go!" he laughs.

"Of course not!" I smile to hide my embarrassment, "Where else would you want to go?"

I quickly change the conversation.

"Berlin would be good," he states.

"Berlin? Lots of sex museums there."

What? What have I just said? Damn you, Discovery Channel, why would air shows about sex in Europe?

"Really? I didn't know," he laughs again, "How about Prague?"

"Sex shops," I state.

"Paris?"

"Orgies."

"Norway?" he laughs.

"Naked people in saunas."

"You seem to know a lot of interesting things about Europe?" his cheeky smile makes me melt.

"I would love to go."

What have I said? I have just come off sounding like a sex fiend.

"Where would you like to go?" Robert leans forward and asks me with his eyes.

"Anywhere in Europe."

Robert reaches his hand forward and touches my hand, sending shivers through my body.

Oh. Wow.

My heart rate beats at the walls of my chest. His hand is so strong yet so soft.

Wow.

I feel my heart beat in my throat.

"Excuse Robert," my moment with Robert is interrupted, "The next scene is ready."

I sip on the milkshake as I watch his cute bottom leave the tent.

He smiles at me as he leaves our private spot, leaving me to finish my strawberry milkshake.

Yum.

And the milkshake is nice too.

Romance: The Billionaire Actor

Chapter 3

The next few hours are a buzz of excitement and adrenalin. My mind is lost in a cloud of passion, reliving my moments with Robert over and over.

I want to tell the world.

I want to put it on the internet and scream to all my friends.

But I shouldn't. I shouldn't tell anyone.

I don't tell my mum. I don't tell my girlfriends. I don't even tell my best friend. They probably won't believe me anyway.

As the hours go past, I can't stop thinking about it. The greatest moment of my life and I can't share it with anyone...

I wander around the movie set in a daze.

But then I see it.

Just when I started to believe that Robert Tatum was genuine, I see something that shatters my belief.

He stands kissing another girl.

Embracing her passionately. Gripping her the way he should be embracing me.

And then another.

He is kissing another girl.

The cameras role all around him, but he kisses her passionately. Embracing her with lust.

Dammit.

I am shattered.

He sucked me in.

He acted his way through our milkshake date. He doesn't want to embrace me. He doesn't want to kiss me.

He is still a player.

He is still a man who gets as many women as he wants.

And he just wanted me to be another one of them.

I want to disappear. I want the world to eat me up.

How could I have been so gullible?

How could I have fallen for the same lines he would have used a thousand times?

I run out of the movie set and run all the way back to my small house - back to my bed - back to the comfort of my warm blankets.

I cry.

And I cry.

And then, I cry some more.

I have to change my pillow a number of times as the tears roll down my face.

How could I have fallen for it?

I should have known it. I should have known that he would have a thousand girls. I should have known that he would have used me.

I am shattered.

I turn on the television as background noise but it is the start of a British romantic comedy movie. I spend the next two hours crying into my pillows, watching the British laugh and romance each other.

After hours of crying, there is a knock at my door.

A heavy, strong knock.

A knock of importance.

But still I ignore it.

I don't want to talk to anyone. Ever again.

But the person is persistent.

I finally rise out of bed, and go to answer the door.

As I open the door, I am surprised.

It is the tall, strong figure of Robert Tatum.

Back at the door to my house.

"Hi," he states.

I don't say anything but I wipe the tears from my eyes.

"Um…" he stumbles over his words, "I just wanted to come pass to say hello."

"Well, you've done that now."

"Ok."

"Ok. Goodbye."

I close the door on the world's most beautiful man.

Knock, knock.

"Yes?" I question as I open the door again.

"Milkshake?"

"No," I shake my head, "That won't work again. I'm not going to be another one of your many girls?"

"Many girls?"

"Why are you questioning me? I saw you. As soon as you left that milkshake date with me, who were smooching every girl in sight."

He shakes his head and whispers, "It's my job."

"Your job?"

"It was part of a scene. Just another scene in a movie. Those girls meant nothing."

"Nothing?"

"It's all part of the movie."

I sniff.

"I would quit it all for you."

This time, I raise my eyebrows, "Me?"

"When I saw you standing on the side of the road as I galloped on that horse, I knew I had to talk to you. Sometimes, when your eyes connect with someone, there is something deeper. Something that can't be put into words. When our eyes connected, I knew that I had to talk to you.

And when we talked, I knew that was it. I have to get to know you better. And I still have to take you for a coffee. And I hear the best coffee in the world is in Europe."

"Europe?"

"Do you want to go to Europe?" he asks.

"Europe?"

"Yeah - sex clubs and museums and prostitutes," he smiles.

Wow. What a smile.

How could I say no to that?

"What about the movie?"

"What movie?"

"This movie?"

"I have two days of shooting left. And that's it. And there are no more kissing scenes."

"Really?"

"Absolutely."

He looks at me.

Not towards me or around me but at me. Straight in the eyes. My heart skips a beat.

Wow.

He is the most beautiful person I have ever seen.

He leans forward – what is he doing?

His lips kiss mine.

It instantly sends me into overdrive. His strong hand reaches up and caresses the side of my face.

Wow.

As he continues to kiss me softly, his hand moves down my body and holds my hips.

I can't resist anymore.

I have to have him.

I grab his strong hand and lead him straight into my lounge room.

As he continues to passionately kiss me, he moves his hands up between my legs, up my skirt. I am so hot.

I can't hold back anymore.

His hand sneaks its way to the top of my thigh, next to my passion. I don't know what to do.

He moves to kissing my neck. Wow. I cannot stop him, he has me sweep away.

He starts to undress me, pulling the jacket from my shoulders. He kisses my collarbone and I suddenly realise that my shirt is gone too. He kisses me back on the lips and I am spinning.

Suddenly, my bra falls off.

Robert stops and rips his shirt off.

Oh wow.

His amazingly cut body is tanned and smooth. His chest is round and curves just below the nipples. His stomach is flat and toned.

I am breathless.

It is everything I ever imagined.

I rub my hands over his chest and I start kiss him back. His chest is like a pack of muscle and I tweak his nipple. Yes.

His hand finds its way back up my skirt. I think about stopping him. But I can't. He has me. I am smitten. I can't stop kissing him back.

His hand touches me. I am instantly wet. I hope that he can't feel that wetness through my underwear. Suddenly, my underwear is on the floor. I don't know how he did that.

He continues to kiss me and he caresses my breasts in a way they have not been handled before. Oh yes, I moan.

He lies me down on the couch and I notice that he is also naked.

I look down at his member. It is big. Very big.

Lying on the couch, his member enters me. He pushes his way in, entering me deep.

My head throws back.

Wow.

Lying on this couch, I have Robert Tatum inside me. Deep, deep inside me. He holds his member in me and I close my eyes. I feel every piece of him, touching me in places I haven't been touched for a long time.

He slowly withdraws and then enters me again. I am so wet. I open my eyes and hold my hands on his chest muscles. Again he slowly withdraws and enters me again.

Wow.

He is so big.

He stands over me missionary style, and I rub my hands up his powerful arms. My hands rub easily over his tanned and smooth body.

He holds himself deep inside me again.

Robert kisses me again and I quickly forget about everything.

He begins to pump me. He thrusts himself hard. Oh yes. He pumps me again. Oh yes.

He is so strong. So deep.

He begins to pump me with rhythm. It sends my head spinning. I become hot as he holds my shoulders and pushes them into the couch. He rams his member into me so deep.

I pant and he growls.

I squirt my juice and this only fuels him to pump harder. Oh yes.

He grabs my legs and moves them up to his shoulders. The back of my legs rest against his body, my feet pointing up in the air. He thrusts himself deep.

Wow.

I have never felt someone so deep. He is reaching into my body, pushing at parts I never knew could be reached. He thrusts himself deep and I squeal loudly.

I enjoy the screaming and I do it again.

This time, I scream louder.

He joins in. He growls loudly, then groans with aggression. He dominates me.

I orgasm.

He pulls his long member from out of me and holds it over my body. He begins to wank his member and I don't know what to do. I lie still.

He scrunches his face in aggression and then explodes over my breasts. Oh wow.

Robert collapses to the couch, his muscles lounging all over my cum stained naked body. We lie in our nakedness for some time, my head floating above the clouds in the buzzing glow of my orgasm.

Oh yes.

"Can we do that in Europe?" he smiles.

"I hope so."

"Then let's do it. Let's do Europe," he smiles again.

I have found all the excitement I ever needed.

Romance: The Billionaire's Mansion

Jodi Cooper

What happens in the mansion stays in the mansion...

Copyright © 2014

Published by Run Free Publishing

All rights reserved.

No part of this publication may be reproduced, stored in a retrieval system, or transmitted, in any form or by any means without the prior permission in writing of the publisher.

Romance: The Billionaire's Mansion

Chapter 1

"Do not talk to him, do not make eye contact and definitely don't drool."

"I'm good with the first two rules but don't drool?"

"Yes. Don't drool, don't stare and absolutely don't fall in love with him. You'll know what I mean when you first see him. Just about every other housecleaner we have hired in the past has broken those first three rules."

"Anything else?"

"Only vacuum the carpet left to right. Start at the left hand side of the room and vacuum to the right hand side. Once who've finished one way, turn the vacuum cleaner off and then take it back to the left hand side and start again."

"That's seems a little odd."

"A lot of things that happen around here are odd. You can afford to be odd when you're one of the richest people in the country. This housecleaning job isn't for everyone. If you don't think you can maintain the confidentiality clause from your work contract, then you should get out before you get in too deep."

"I don't remember signing any clause like that yesterday."

"Don't you read what you're given?"

"Not really…"

"Well, you should. One of the things that you had to sign was the confidentiality clause. If you break it, then you could be liable for fines up to half a million dollars."

"Really? Is it lawful to have a clause like that?"

"You signed it."

"I signed a lot of paperwork yesterday. I must have signed fifty different sheets. I read the first few pages but after that I was just adding my name to a page. Fifty pages is a lot of reading for a housecleaning job. But is the fine really worth half a million dollars?"

Anna nods, "Tyson Watson takes his confidentiality very seriously. Actually, he seems to take most things very seriously."

"So what sort of secrets is he hiding in this mansion?"

"There are rumours…"

"About?"

"Special rooms."

"And what happens in these special rooms?"

"The rumour is…"

Anna stops mid-sentence with her jaw dropping almost to the floor. I turn to look at what has shocked her and I see a tall man with broad shoulders smoothly waltz into the room.

It has to be him.

Tyson Watson.

He walks past, barely acknowledging our existence, until he stops and stares at my breasts. He does not even try to conceal the blatant perve.

"Are you the new maid?" he finally looks up at my face.

"Yes," I stammer, "I'm here to do a great job of cleaning your house."

"Cleaning my house?" he laughs, "I hope you do a great job too. But not of cleaning my house."

I'm confused. I must have missed something. It could have been in those fifty pages I signed yesterday.

"And what's your name?"

"Kate," I smile.

"Pleased to meet you, Kate," he holds out his large hand, "I'm glad you want to do a great job."

His smile is disarming, almost cheeky. His eyes stare straight into mine, nearly making me melt into a puddle of mess.

"Pleased to meet you, sir," I stammer again. I feel like I should courtesy in the introduction.

He is more attractive and more seductive than anyone I have ever met.

"And what is your experience, Kate?"

"I have worked…"

He laughs out-loud.

"No, I don't mean your work experience. What is your life experience?"

"Um… I'm not sure what you're referring too, sir."

"Please, don't call me sir. Call me Tyson."

"I'd call you hot but if you want to be called Tyson, that's ok too," I smile.

The smile on his face stretches further, "And I'd call you sexy, but that may be inappropriate for an employee."

"It could be seen as harassment…" I continue.

"Well, I'll word up my lawyer for a harassment case then, because things are going to go a lot further than that."

He takes a moment before leaving the room, his eyes clearly undressing me. He looks at me from top to bottom, looking at my every curve.

His towering frame exits through the foyer of his large mansion, and into the next room.

"Oh my," Anna smiles.

I take a few moments to watch his cute round bottom walk away before I let out a sigh of lust.

"Tell me, Kate, what made you want this job?" Anna asks.

"The money. The pay is extraordinarily good for a cleaner."

"The rumours didn't worry you?"

"I haven't heard the rumours."

"You haven't worked in the cleaning industry long, have you?"

"I cleaned a few times at college but I have been working in a stockbroking firm for the last few years. They went bust and jobs are hard to come by."

"So you came back to cleaning?"

"With pay like this, why wouldn't you?"

Anna nods, "Just watch yourself. It's clear that he really likes you. I could tell that from the moment he set eyes on you. So just watch yourself in this house - especially when Tyson is around."

Anna gives me a look of cheekiness and leaves me to clean the foyer spotless.

The little flirt with a billionaire distracts my mind while I spend the next few hours wiping the grand staircase, window frames and doors.

Romance: The Billionaire's Mansion

Chapter 2

"You can tell those bastards that I'm coming to their office next week. And they'd better have a good offer on the table – or we walk away."

Those are Tyson's last comments for the phone conversion.

"Can't get a moment to myself," he mumbles as he puts the phone down next to the pool chair. He is topless, exposing his toned and strong body to me, sunning himself next to the large pool.

As he starts to relax, my figure catches his eyes. My tight little skirt is highlighted by the afternoon sun.

"Hello," I greet him.

"Hi."

An awkward silence drifts over us.

"The garden looks good," I compliment him.

"Does it?" he questions.

"Um... yes. You don't think so?"

Tyson looks around the garden - the beautiful hedges, the beautiful rows of flowers and the stunningly perfect green grass.

"I suppose it does."

"You suppose?"

"Yes. I haven't really had much time to look at it. Although at this moment I lay sunning myself on a lounge next to the pool, this is the first time I have to my weekend house in months. Weeks of work turned into months, and months turned into years. I think I am physically and emotionally drained," Tyson sighs tiredly, "I had told the office that I wasn't going to take any calls today but this was urgent. It's always urgent. But this is my life. Meetings, decisions, phone calls and travel. It never switches off."

"Sounds tough."

"Don't get me wrong, Kate. I have a lot of stuff. But I've also made a lot of sacrifices. And it's those sacrifices that have made me a lot of money."

"But the same sacrifices also mean that you no longer have a ring on his finger?"

I can clearly see the tan line of where a ring used to be on his left hand.

"It's lonely being at the top. Not that he had a lot of time to worry about that."

"You should always make time to smell the roses," I smile.

"That's quite sage advice," Tyson is drawn in by my smile. It usually my smile that draws them in.

"Opportunities don't come around very often, you have to take every opportunity available," I continue.

Tyson acknowledges my advice with a smirk and a shrug of the shoulders, "How can I help you Kate?"

"I'm giving the pool area a wipe down and I just need to clean under this chair," I continue pointing to the chair next to Tyson.

I walk to the chair and bend from the hips in-front of Tyson, pointing my pert bottom to his view.

Tyson can't help but watch. His eyes are drawn to my behind and I catch him staring,

"Do you like what you see?"

Tyson nods, "I just couldn't see a knickers line in your skirt."

"That's because I'm not wearing any," I smile.

"Well…." Tyson is lost for words.

I bend down again and run my hand up my left leg until it reaches the top of my thigh. Tyson sits up, paying full attention.

I can tell he wants me. The bulge in his shorts makes that clear.

I move towards Tyson and rest my hand on his strong chest. I push him back down on his pool chair, until he is lying backwards. His eyes are attached to my movements, watching my every move very closely. I lift one leg over his crotch and straddle him, running my hands over his white polo shirt. Tyson reaches up and begins to unbutton my shirt, exposing a perky pair of breasts.

I throw my blouse to the side of the pool chair and he quickly undoes my bra. Tyson's hands clutch at my perkiness, his hands rubbing all over breasts. His eyes do not move from my breasts.

I begin to feel the pulsating manhood between my legs. It is pushing up at me. I can feel it become harder and harder the longer he plays with my breasts.

Biting my bottom lip, I reach down and undo his belt, running my hand down his shorts. Tyson is lost for words.

I pull out his member and move down to his legs, holding his hard member in my right hand. I gently run my hand up and down the member, looking up as Tyson moans in pleasure. Gently, I place my tongue around the tip of his manliness. Running my tongue around his hardness, he groans in pleasure.

I suddenly swallow him whole and he groans in his deep, manly voice. I continue to rub his hard, big cock as I hold him in my mouth.

He is so big. So manly.

My hand stretches around his shaft, gripping it tightly.

I stand up, hitch my skirt and straddle my pussy over his hard cock. My wetness touches his cock, tempting him. He wants me. He wants to be inside me.

I sit on him whole. Tyson groans loudly in pleasure.

Resting my hands on his strong chest, I rotate my hips on his manhood. His hands play with my perky breasts again as I move my hips in a circle motion. I run my fingers into his mouth and he bites on them with pleasure. I thrusts my hips back and forth on his cock as he begins to push upwards into my.

But I stop.

I want him to dominate me. I want this billionaire to show me whose boss.

Climbing off Tyson, I bend over the pool chair next to him, pointing my pussy to his will.

"Fuck me hard, big boy."

He obliges, standing and entering his large cock into my wet pussy, pushing himself deep inside me. I yelp as he is touching me in all the right places.

His large hands hold my behind and he begins to slowly enter in and out of me.

He continues slowly, tempting me with his strength.

"Harder!" I demand.

He obeys, slamming his cock aggressively into and out of my wetness. His cock is wide, stretching my pussy lips, bringing me to orgasm quickly. He continues to pump me, ramming himself deep inside.

In the blistering sunshine, in the middle of the open air, I orgasm.

I scream to the gardens.

"Yes!"

He groans.

He pumps.

He holds my hips tightly, in full control of my movements. I try to move back on him but he forces me forward. Tyson reaches forward and grabs my ponytail, pulling at it hard.

"Yes!" I scream louder.

He pulls my hair tighter as he pumps me with his cock.

I feel him come.

He unleashes a last burst of energy into me, then pulls out and lies on the pool chair, his face looking up towards the sky, a smile drifting across his face.

"Wow," he pants.

I fall to the other chair, taking a moment to calm the spinning orgasm.

When I settle, I pick up my blouse and I wink at him, "Excuse me sir, I have some cleaning to do."

"Wait."

I stop and look back at my new lover.

"What are you doing tomorrow night?"

"Cleaning your big house."

"I am hosting a ball here tomorrow night. Please come."

"A ball? I'm not sure I would fit in at ball? It's not my sort of scene."

"You are beautiful enough to fit in anywhere."

"Thankyou but I have nothing to wear at such short notice."

"Don't worry about that. I'll look after you. And don't worry about the dress, I'll get my personal assistant to give you a dress. She'll call you within the hour."

"Um…" I want to say no purely out of nerves.

"You can't say no," he reads my mind, "It's settled. You'll be here at the ball tomorrow night."

Hot damn. This could very well be the moment that changes my life.

Romance: The Billionaire's Mansion

Chapter 3

As the hours tick past, Tyson is all I can think about. He consumes my every thought, and I wrongly blurt out his name in a number of situations. He has me smitten.

All night I toss and turn. I can't sleep as my heart rate is going through the roof.

What a beautiful man.

He is the most beautiful man I have ever been with, or seen. Despite Anna's earlier warning, he has stolen my heart.

When the sun finally rises the next morning, I sigh with relief. The time when I get to see him again is closer. I really can't wait to see him again. I really can't wait to kiss him again.

As the morning slowly creeps past, nerves fill everything that I do. Tyson's personal assistant calls and I provide her with my measurements. Within the hour a courier has arrived with strapless dress at my front door. I thank him and run into my bedroom to try it on.

It is an amazing dress and fits my curves perfectly. Despite being a little too revealing for my liking, it is the most beautiful dress I have ever worn. The fabric feels so wonderful on my skin. After the initial excitement starts to pass, I catch a glimpse of the designer name stitched into the inside hem. It is not someone I have heard of before, so I quickly do an internet search on the name.

Oh my. The designer's website is full of pictures of celebrities walking down red carpets in their clothing. This designer must be special.

I try the dress on numerous times and spend most of the morning looking into the mirror. The dress makes me feel amazing and special. I feel beautiful and wonderful. The dress makes me feel confident and sexy. I love it.

The hours of the day fly past as nervously fiddle about. I have been told not to come into work today but I'll still get paid.

I suppose that's one of the bonuses when you share a moment with your boss...

After way too long staring in the mirror, I am relieved when the ride arrives to take me to the ball. The clean, black limousine arrives perfectly on time. I have never ridden in a limousine before and I am stunned by its look of luxury. As I walk towards it, I catch a glimpse of my reflection in the shiny car. Wow, this dress makes me look good.

The limousine driver is a nice, older man with a charming smile. He holds the door open for me has I sit inside, "You look lovely today, ma'am. That is a very nice dress."

"Thankyou," I smile as I slide onto the back seat.

The leather seats of the limousine are more comfortable than my bed. Actually, the whole car is probably the size of half my house. And it would be worth a lot more.

As the driver sits back in to drive me to the ball, I ask what he knows about Tyson and he smiles.

"Tyson is interesting character," he avoids my question.

"He has a big house," I state.

"That is one of his houses – yes."

Oh wow. Who is this man?

"How long have you been driving for him?"

"Over ten years now. He is a very good boss. He looks after us all."

"I love his mansion. How long has he had that place?"

"He bought that place about two years ago. That place comes with one rule though."

"And what's that rule?"

"What happens in the mansion stays in the mansion."

With that, the driver ominously closes the window between the front seat and the back seat of the limousine.

What have I gotten myself into?

The car drives up to the house that I was cleaning barely twenty-four hours earlier. It looks more impressive than I first thought. I had thought that it looked impressive from the staff entrance but the guest entrance is even more so. Its grandeur shines through from this entrance.

As I walk into the foyer, I can't help but see a spot of dust that I must have missed yesterday. I sneak across and discreetly rub the spot with my hand.

I enter the large and impressive ballroom in the most beautiful cocktail dress I have ever worn, but I still feel really out of place with this group of people. There are some amazingly beautiful people here. Everyone else seems really comfortable mingling and chatting. I don't know what to do, so I nervously stand at one side of the room, sipping at a champagne glass.

When Tyson enters the room, everyone else looks at him. Like a rockstar starting a concert, he is the centre of attention. His stature among these people is obviously great.

He thanks a few people for coming, shakes a number of hands, kisses a couple girls on the cheek and then walks over to me.

"I am very happy that you made it."

"Thankyou. I'm very happy to be here."

"That's a lovely dress. I like it a lot."

"Thankyou again. Your personal assistant arranged it very quickly once I supplied her with my measurements."

"Of course, the dress would look a lot better on the floor of my bedroom," he whispers in my ear.

"I think that it would match the carpet of your office better."

He smiles and looks around the room.

"You'd better meet me in the office at the top of the stairs in ten minutes then," he whispers in my ear again.

He provides me with a wink as he starts to mingle with the rest of the crowd.

Is he serious?

I really hope so.

That tuxedo looks so good on him.

I drink the rest of my champagne, and walk up the grand stairs to look for the office. It's easy to get lost in this mansion. I may have seen the office yesterday but there are so many doors, it is really easy to choose the wrong one.

I find the right door, gently push it open and find the dark room. I am still stunned by the size of it. The ceiling is high enough to fit another floor inside.

I wait in the darkness, leaning on the office table in my elegant red cocktail dress.

I'm so nervous, do I wait for him? Is he worth waiting for? What if he's not interested?

This time I will seduce him. I will take him.

But what if he rejects me? Is it worth the risk of rejection?

I think about his kiss. His muscles. His smile.

Oh yes. It is worth it.

I hear a quiet knock on the door. Those ten minutes have flown by very quickly.

Tyson smiles as he enters, his beautiful eyes shining through the darkness. I stand from the desk and walk over, closing the door and discreetly locking it.

My heart is in my mouth. It is beating so hard. My arms are weak with nerves.

I touch his hand.

He looks at me.

I run my hand up his thigh. His beautiful eyes gaze at me and I can see the bulge in his pants grow.

I reach up and kiss him. His lips are so soft, so tender, so juicy. Passion fills the air. The room is alight with chemistry.

I push him back until he rest on the armchair at the side of the room. I want him in my mouth. I want to eat all of him.

When he sits down, I unzip his pants and his member instantly jumps out like an unleashed tiger. It is so firm.

I put it in my mouth. He is big. And strong. I love it. It tastes fresh, manly.

I run my mouth over and over his member and it grows harder with each stroke. He clenches and moans. He is ready to cum.

I pinch the head of his penis with two fingers. He's not going yet. It will not be this quick.

He smirks.

I pull down my stockings and knickers whilst he stares in awe. I love his wide-eyed lust. I push my hand against his chest and feel all of his strength.

Hitching my dress up, I spread my legs over his seated body. He sits ready and hard.

I hold his cock in my hand and place my pussy lips at the top of his member. It feels so right. I hold and let my wet pussy juice flow over his strong piece.

I hesitate and he almost explodes in anticipation.

My pussy swallows his hard piece inside me in one go. We both hold our breath in lust. When I move my hips I feel him so deep inside me. I feel every part of his perfectly shaped member inside my pussy.

I am dripping wet.

I place my finger inside his mouth and his sweet lips lap on my finger as I swivel my hips on the chair.

He moans loudly and I start to bounce.

My thighs push me up and down, and his long member is so hard inside me. I grab the back of his strong neck for support, and my other hand reaches behind me and grabs his thigh.

He forcibly pulls my breasts out of my dress and he nuzzles his face into my breasts, kissing as I bounce.

I squeal.

I feel his warmth squirt inside me and I squeal again.

I stop bouncing and lean forward, resting my head against his manly chest.

We both take more than a few moments to catch our breath, buzzing in the feeling of ecstasy.

Sensational.

After a few minutes of silence have pasted, I stand off him, taking his member from out of me, and pull on my stockings. He stands, zips his pants and smiles.

"I best get back to mingling," he states.

"Wait, when will I see you again?" I ask.

He smiles, "Do you like to clean?"

"Um... yes. It's what you pay me for."

"Good. When you come to work tomorrow, tell Anna that you have been instructed to clean the special room..."

Romance: The Billionaire's Mansion

Chapter 4

I feel like Cinderella.

After my night of passion with Tyson, I am back to mopping the floors of his grand house. As I mop and clean, I think about Tyson. I think about his toned body, his smell, his eyes and his charm. It is everything that I ever imagined.

Perfect.

After half an hour cleaning, Anna finally arrives at work.

"Anna," I grab her.

"Yes? What's wrong?"

"I have been asked by Tyson to clean the special room?"

"The special room? Already?"

I nod.

"What's the special room?"

"He must really like you, Kate," Anna smiles.

"Is it part of the rumours that you were going to tell me about?"

She takes me aside to where no-one else can hear us, "Cleaning the special room comes with rules."

"Ok. What are they?"

"One – what happens in there stays in there. You are not allowed to talk to anyone ever about the special room. The rule of the mansion is 'What happens in the mansion stays in the mansion' but what happens in that room doesn't go any further than those walls."

"Really? What happens in there? Have you been in there?"

Anna shakes her head, "He asked me once but I said no. I'd heard the rumours. And after I said no, he asked me to 'manage' who cleans the room."

"Do many people clean the room?"

"No. He's only had two people clean it before. They no longer work here."

"What happens in there, Anna?"

"Rule two," Anna deliberately ignores my question, "Keep an open mind. Be willing to do whatever happens. If you don't think that your mind is open then I would recommend quitting this job now. Don't go into the room if you're not willing to experience something new."

"Rule three?"

"Green trees."

"Green trees? What does 'green trees' have to do with anything?"

"Nothing."

"Then why is it a rule?"

"You'll see. But don't forget 'green trees'. It is probably the most important words that you'll know over the next day. Repeat the word for me."

"Green trees. Right. Don't forget 'green trees'."

"Do you know how to get to the wine cellar?"

I nod.

"The room is at the back of the wine cellar," Anna continues, "You have to walk through the cellar and there is a door that is past the back of the last line of wine barrels. You can't see the door unless you've past the wine barrels."

"Is the door locked?"

"The key is hanging on the back of the last wine barrel. You need to start cleaning it at twelve o'clock."

I nod, "That's only ten minutes away."

"Then you'd better start walking down there."

I turn and begin to walk nervously away from Anna.

"And Kate," she stops me, "Good luck."

I'm not sure about this.

I'm really not sure about this…

The walk into the wine cellar is long and dark. Tyson made me nervous enough without this level of mystery. His eyes and good looks were enough to get my heart racing but this is another level.

This is actually scary.

I think about turning back but everytime I do, I can smell his smell and taste his lips. That is worth the risk.

I slowly walk down into the dark wine cellar, and the automatic lights turn on with my entrance. The cellar is cold, long and dimly lit, and I navigate through the rows of bottled wine and barrels. The amount of wine in this room must be worth a lot of money.

The last wine barrel covers the entrance to a large wooden door. The door looks ominous. My heart is racing as I stare at the door.

Do I go in?

Am I prepared for whatever happens in here?

I'm not prepared.

But I look for the key anyway. I find the key hanging on the back of the wine barrel, and I fumble it into the door. I hold the key in the door before turning it and contemplate how I have found myself here.

I saw the ad online while searching for work. It was almost too good to be true. Great pay for cleaning a house. I had to send in a picture of myself with the job application, which is unusual for a cleaning job. When the job offer came through, I wanted to say no. The great pay for a cleaning job seemed a little suspicious but it's hard to say no when it seems so easy.

I am an educated and skilled individual but I have been without work for too long. I lost my job when the stockbroking firm I worked for closed down, as did a lot of businesses. It's hard to find work when no-one is hiring. There aren't many jobs in my industry at the moment and I had to look elsewhere to see what I can do.

I had done some cleaning jobs to get me through college but turning to cleaning was a last resort.

And the bills just keep piling up. They just kept coming. I got accustomed to a nice lifestyle and I always thought the work would come back.

But the work didn't come back.

So this was my last resort.

After a few glasses of wine, I responded to the online advert. I wrote a brief application and sent in four pictures of myself, as requested.

Within a day I received a list of instructions, a contract that was much too long to read, and a pay offer that I couldn't refuse.

I tried to say no. I tried to find a reason why I shouldn't do this job - but I couldn't. I knew something was unusual about the job.

So, I guess I'm about to find out how unusual it is…

Romance: The Billionaire's Mansion

Chapter 5

As I turn the key to the heavy wooden door, my heart starts to pound at the walls of my chest.

The butterflies fill my stomach.

A few more moments pass before I decide to enter.

Walking into the dark room, my mouth drops open in shock.

Oh no.

I don't know where to look first.

At the handcuffs hanging from the ceiling or the four-poster bed with ties on each post?

At leather suits hanging on the wall or the cage at the side?

At the array of sex toys laid out on the shelving or the whips on the wall?

It is a sensory overload.

Then there is the machine that I don't even know what it does.

I walk towards the machine, which looks like a red rocking horse with straps. I run my hand along it and look at my finger.

There is no dust on it.

A room under a house like this would gather dust. It has obviously been cleaned not long ago.

Which means that I haven't been sent down here to clean.

My heart skips a beat.

What have I gotten myself into?

"Hello."

The voice scares me. It is the deep, dominant voice of Tyson, standing at the entrance to the room.

"I see that you decided to come down here, Kate."

"Why am I here? This room doesn't need cleaning."

"It might in an hour or so," he smiles cheekily.

Damn it. His smile is so disarming. His voice is safe. I'm not sure I want to do this but to him, I can't say no. He has my heart and lust.

I'll do anything for him.

"Do you know what that machine is for?" he asks me.

"No," I reply nervously, "I've never seen anything like."

"That's a pity."

"What's it used for?"

"I don't know," he laughs, "I ordered it from Amsterdam but it didn't come with instructions. I haven't been able to figure it out yet."

My tension is obvious, my hands are shaking slightly as I touch the machine.

"I like the handcuffs though," he states as he runs his hands on the cuffs from the roof.

"You do?"

"Well, they would look a lot better if you were in them."

That makes me instantly wet. Whether it is the nerves or it is Tyson sexiness, I am excited. Very excited.

I have never done anything like this before, but with Tyson - I feel safe.

I want to do it with him. I want him to dominate me. I want him to tie me up.

I want this.

I want him.

He looks at me, "Undress."

"You want me to undress?"

He nods.

It takes a moment for the request to sink in and I nervously stand my ground.

"Undress," he requests again.

This time I do as I'm told. I take off my shirt, pull down my skirt, and kick off my shoes. I stand in my lacy underwear, ready for the next request.

"Everything. Take off everything."

I pause.

He nods.

I can't resist. He has a power over me that I can't explain. I unclip my bra and pull down my knickers, leaving my naked body standing, exposed, in this dungeon.

Tyson watches my body move as I undress. He smiles when I am naked.

"Now, come here," he states with one hand on the handcuffs that dangle from the roof.

Naked, I apprehensively walk across, where he is holding out his hand for me to put mine in. I give him my hand and he guides it up to cuffs hanging from the roof.

As my hands are clipped in, the shaking stops. Tyson's warm hands are caring but dominant, loving but superior. This is dangerous but I feel safe with Tyson.

But turned on at the same time…

"Do you remember what Anna told you?"

"Yes," I nod.

'Green trees'.

Don't forget 'green trees'.

Suddenly, the straps that are holding my hands are pulled tight, and my feet come off the ground. I am dangling by my arms, held in place by leather handcuffs.

To relieve the pressure from my arms sockets, Tyson places a step under my feet, "You can stand on there for a minute."

He smiles and starts to undress himself as he walks over to the 'work bench'. He whips off his shirt and shows off his large and strong shoulders, and when he pulls down his pants, I see that cute behind in all its glory.

Oh, I'm wet in anticipation.

What is he reaching for?

He grabs something off the bench and I see that it is a large plastic dildo. He turns around and I get to see that toned set of abs again. Yum.

Standing in the room with a large smile and a large dildo, he looks sexy. Both of them turn me on. He walks back over and runs his hand up my thigh and onto my wetness. I don't know why he's bothering with the lubricant, I am wet enough.

As I hang naked in the middle of the room, with my hands tied to the ceiling, his fingers slide up the inside of my leg and up to my pussy. He slides his fingers in, but he takes them back out and into his mouth. He sucks the juices off his fingers and runs the dildo over my perky breasts. My nipples are so hard.

I feel the dildo slide into me and it stretches my pussy lips. I like that. I like the sensation of pain shooting through my body. I like it a lot.

After gently caressing the dildo into and out of me, he holds it all the way in. Oh, that feels good.

Suddenly, he jams the dildo into me with passion and aggression. Gritting his teeth, he pumps it upwards into me. He muscles flex as he rams it hard into me. It forces me to scream loudly and passionately.

"Yes!!!!"

As soon as he sees me enjoying it, he stops.

Smiling at my frustration, he is enjoying himself. If I could take my hands out of these ties, I would. I would ravish his hot body. But they have been tied tightly to the roof. I struggle and he can see me struggle.

"Put it in me," I state.

His smile is almost dismissive.

"Put it in me!" I demand.

"When I'm ready, Kate, when I'm ready," he smiles cheekily.

He walks around me, running his hands all over my sensitive parts. His hand runs up the back of my legs and up my butt. He runs his hand down my crack and it sends shivers through me. He knows all my sensitive spots. He knows the spots that make me squirm. And he uses it to his advantage. His hand runs over my bottom, touching all the right spots.

Slap.

Ouch.

He spanks my behind hard.

Very hard.

I feel my bottom tingle with the slap, sending the sensation through my whole being. It hurts – but strangely - I like it.

I like it a lot.

The second slap comes down with thunderous force, connecting with my raw skin. I yell in pain but I am surprised at how it fuels my passion.

I growl with gritted teeth.

I have never growled before.

I really am surprised at how primal I feel.

He slaps again.

"Harder," I tell him.

Why did I say that?

Because I want him to spank me harder.

He slaps hard.

Yes please.

The more he slaps, the more I want it. The more he slaps, the more he wants to.

"Harder, Tyson, harder," I growl.

He unleashes two quick slaps on my butt and I grip the cuffs with all my might. I growl again. I want him to punish me.

Slap.

Oh. Yes.

He pauses and runs his hands all over my body. His touch is strong. Wow. I feel so wet already. I feel the softness of tender lips kiss my sore butt, making me even wetter. Oh yes.

"Now Kate, I'm going to fuck you."

Yes please.

As he walks around the front of me, I notice that he is naked and his member is sitting stiff and upright. I lift my legs over his shoulders until my pussy is in-front of his face. He pulls me up and begins to lick my wetness. My legs wrap around his head and I thrust on his tongue. I moan loudly with passion as my bottom rests on his chest. He lashes his tongue onto me with primal passion. His strong hands hold my bottom up and his touch sends my head spinning. He is a very talented man with a very talented tongue.

He moves me back down until my ankles are the only thing left on his shoulders. My arms are dangling from the roof and my legs are dangling from his shoulders. My pussy is sitting at the perfect height for entry, wet and ready. He holds me tight and slides his hard member into me. He thrusts his heavy cock deep into me.

Oh, that feels so good. It feels amazing. He pounds his hard cock into me and I dangle like a piece of meat being used for his satisfaction. I squirm and lash around with primal aggression but he holds me tight.

He is in complete control. Owning me, he thrusts with aggression. There are moments where the positions are awkward, but it doesn't stop the passion.

His hard cock is touching me places that I didn't know I had. It is touching my perfect spots. I love it.

He thrusts hard again and then he stops.

Smiling, he lowers my legs but leaves me hanging for a few moments, letting the juices run down the inside of my leg.

But he is not finished with me yet.

He walks back over to his bench and returns with a small piece of black cloth. He wraps the cloth around my eyes, and suddenly everything is dark. It is a thick blindfold but I like it.

He uncuffs my hands, leaving me blindfolded but naked and free.

"Lick my balls," he demands in his deep voice.

I kneel and he puts his member in front of my face. I feel my hands over his member and I lash my tongue on his balls. He is shaved and full. Full and ready to explode. I hold his member in my hands as I run my tongue all over his smooth sack. He moans with delight.

"Now lick my anal," he demands again.

I move my tongue and my fingers across to his anal, pushing my index finger in and licking his anal. I feel a gentle whip on my back - his way of making sure I continue to do as I'm told.

I don't know what's going to happen next but I have to remember the safe word – 'Green trees'.

Green trees, green trees, green trees – I keep telling myself.

His butt clenches tighter the further I push my fingers in.

He pulls away and leads my hands back to the straps hanging from the ceiling. He ties me in tight and I don't have much room to move. This time, my feet stand flat on the ground with my legs spread wide. His hands run over my legs, down to my ankles and he locks them into place with another set of straps.

Here I stand, strapped into place, my naked body exposed to the will of this man that I hardly even know. Even if I said the safe word, I don't know if he'll stop. Will he stop? I start to become nervous as he runs his tongue all over my naked body.

I quickly become lost in his lustful passion, his wet mouth kissing my breasts. He runs his hands over my body over and over again. Running his hand between my legs to the top of my thighs, but not quite touching my pussy.

I become very wet. I love the way he adores my female body, my curves. I try to grab him with my hands but my arms are locked into place. I moan as his hand finally touches my wetness again.

His fingers enter me. He is in complete control of me. I can feel him so deep. I feel his fingers dance inside my pussy and I squirm my hips around his hand.

He licks my face and kisses my breasts. He controls me. I have no control over him. He controls me completely. Suddenly, I feel my pussy lips stretch. He bends down and I think he forces his whole hand into me. My eyes nearly roll back in my head. Wow.

That hurts.

But as he gently rocks his hand in and out, I love it. His mouth moves down to my clit and his tongue starts to dance on my spot. He knows the exact spot to touch me. With his hand inside me and his tongue touching me, it sends me into a spin.

I start to feel dizzy and I pull at the straps hard, trying to get out. I can't. I'm trapped. I want to stop. But I love it. It is sending me off to another place. I don't know if I want to allow myself to go there. But I can't stop it.

I feel my arms start to shake and hotness overcomes me. I scream with passion and pain. I am sent on a trip. He is jamming his hand into and out of me when I explode with juices over his arm. He slows and continues to rub, but soon he stands up.

My mind is a daze with ecstasy.

He grabs my face and forces his tongue down my throat.

When he is finished kissing me, he unties my arms and legs and leads me over to bench. He pushes me forward from the hips and ties my hands to the end of the bench. My feet, still touching the ground, are strapped in as well.

I am in a complete daze of ecstasy. I could be led anywhere at this point.

I do not even know if I can comprehend what is happening.

I feel a cold liquid spread over my behind and he rubs his fingers into my ass. His member feels its way to the spot and forces its way in. Again, I groan with pain and delight.

He rams himself into my ass with force, slapping my cheeks with passion. He continues to slap and I continue to groan. Pain is spinning me to another place. I am almost unconscious with the pain but I love it. I am orgasming like I've never done before.

It is amazing.

I am in another place.

I am so high that I do not even notice him stop.

I just notice him untie my hands and legs.

I do not know how long I lay in that same position for, but I am lost in the moment.

Time stands still.

He leaves the room without saying another word but I lie on the bench for some time. I lie in the buzz and glow of my moment.

Wow.

Yes.

When I finally move, I am in pain. My pussy and my butt have been stretched and I struggle to walk.

But I love it.

It takes me more than an hour before I decide to get dressed. Finally, I start to come down from the dizzying heights of the best orgasm of my life.

Reality starts to set back in.

When I go back upstairs from the cellar, I expect Tyson to be gone.

But he isn't.

Instead, he is standing at the top of the stairs with a two large glasses of wine, and he hands one to me.

"I have been waiting for you."

"I'm sorry. I took my time coming up the stairs..."

"No. I have been waiting for you my whole life."

I smile.

"That was the best sex of my life," I state.

He smiles, "Good."

"When can we do it again?" I ask.

"I don't want to do this to you again."

"Why not? Didn't you enjoy it?" I am shocked. He clearly enjoyed it.

"I loved it. That was amazing."

"Then what's wrong?"

"You."

"What's wrong with me?"

"Nothing. That's the problem. I enjoy your company more than I enjoy the sex. I have never been able to say that before. And I think that's a lot more important than a sexual fantasy."

I nod, "But I really enjoyed it..."

"This mansion is my play house. I don't want you living here with me."

"Ok…" my disappointment is clear.

"No. I want you to move in with me into my city penthouse."

"Really?"

"Absolutely. You are something else. You are amazing. I want you around me all the time. I need you in the city with me. I have never felt a connection like this before."

"On one condition," I state.

"And what's that?"

"Only if we can come back here for holidays…"

He smiles, "As you wish."

Romance: The Billionaire's Assistant

Jodi Cooper

Copyright © 2014

Published by Run Free Publishing

All rights reserved.

No part of this publication may be reproduced, stored in a retrieval system, or transmitted, in any form or by any means without the prior permission in writing of the publisher.

Romance: The Billionaire's Assistant

Chapter 1

I need this job.

I really need this job.

I sit in the waiting room of the 52nd floor on this new inner-city skyscraper, my knees twitching up and down with nerves. I have applied for a job as a personal assistant to the manager and owner of the largest property development firm in the country. A job like this could set my career up. If I can show that I can hold onto this job, then I should be able to land any job I want in the future.

I have read every tip on how to perform well in a high pressure job interview but nothing prepares you for the nerves. I am so nervous that I even think about walking away. But no, this opportunity is too good. I have to give it a go.

This is my chance of a lifetime.

"Russel White will see you now," a nice young lady instructs me and holds out her arm, pointing into the office.

I stand, fix my tight business skirt and enter the manager's office.

Wow.

What a room. Floor to ceiling windows all around – looking down on the city below. The office has all the modern furnishings and a lot of space. Very, very impressive.

"Hello."

Oh wow.

I am a bit stunned. I expected the room to look good but I didn't expect this.

I didn't expect my interviewer to be so good looking. I thought maybe he would be an old man with grey hair and smelling of old man aftershave. Instead he is stunning. A beautiful smile, beautiful skin, and an amazingly fitted suit.

Wow.

"I'm Russel White. Pleased to meet you, Karen. Please have a seat."

I sit and I realise that mouth is still open in shock.

He nods as he sits back down and waits for me to respond.

"Hi."

Hi? That's all I can say? I am in an interview to the greatest job in my life and all I can say is hi?

"Hi," he repeats uncomfortably, "Tell me about yourself, Karen."

"Um… hi."

What? Come on, Karen, pull yourself together!

"I have been working as a personal assistant to the manager at 'Tovo Computing' for the past two years," I finally start to get my words out.

"Ok. Tell me about your role?"

Again I freeze.

His deep blue eyes are looking at me, waiting for an answer. His eyes look straight at me. Not around me, not through me but straight at me. I am smitten. A job interview is hard enough without having to do it in-front of the most beautiful man I have ever seen.

"Um... I was assisting the manager and learning about the direction of the company."

"And what direction was that?"

"Up."

He laughs.

Whew.

"And what are you looking for in this role?"

"I'm really looking for someone to guide me through the rigours of business," I start to loosen up, "I want to learn about the business while servicing my boss. I'm here to work hard and do things right."

He nods.

"Thanks, Karen. If I decide to take you on, I'll be in contact over the next week."

That's it?

"You didn't want to ask any more questions?"

"No, thankyou. I have already made my decision."

Dammit.

I smile and nod, leaving the beautiful man sitting in his beautiful office.

I forget about the job interview over the next couple of weeks and return to my current mundane job. I acknowledge that I blew the interview. He didn't want to know me or my history. Managing a company like that, he wouldn't have the time to mess about.

I guess first impressions really do count. I guess that it really is those first few moments that make or break an interview. But then the phone rings.

I start on Monday.

I can't believe it.

The job of a lifetime is mine.

Personal assistant to a Billionaire.

Romance: The Billionaire's Assistant

Chapter 2

After two days of orientation, I finally get to sink my teeth into the role of personal assistant to Mr White.

He is amazing. So impressive.

He controls meetings, controls the business and controls my heart. When he talks, people listen. When a decision to be made, he swift and confident. If there is a disagreement, he listens. Then he knocks the others flat. I am so impressed by Russel.

And then there are his looks.

Every day he is dressed in another tailored suit. He stands tall and confident. His personal grooming is immaculate. Tall with broad shoulders and impossibly good looks – when he smiles I almost fall apart.

During the first week, I spend my time printing and faxing, organising meetings and organising people. I love the importance of working for Russel. In-between meetings, he takes the time to inform me of the basics of the business.

"Karen?" he calls out from inside his office to my desk just outside his office doors.

"Yes?" I walk in.

"Did you have a look at the Building Plan paper that asked you to have a look at yesterday?"

"Um… yes. I read through that last night."

"Good. What do you think?"

"What do I think about what?"

"What do you think about the building plan?"

"I think it was good."

"And the decisions that need to be made?"

"What about the decisions?"

"Would you go ahead with the building plan."

"Yes. I would."

"Ok, why?"

"I think they were sound. I think the plan covered all bases but I think the major risk is approval from the local groups."

"Good," he nods confidently.

He takes a moment - pauses - and then picks up the phone, "John, go ahead with the building plan. We've identified that the key risk is getting approval from the local groups."

He hangs up the phone.

"What did you think of the paper?" I ask.

"I didn't read it."

Oh my. He has just approved a building plan based on my recommendation.

Wow.

He stands from behind his desk and confidently walks over to his drink cabinet.

"Glass of pinot?"

"Pinot?"

"Red wine."

"Sure."

Great, I have really shown my class now.

He hands me the glass and I sip at the beautiful red wine.

"Wow," I comment, "That is the best wine I have ever tasted."

"It should be. It's a few thousand dollars a bottle."

My eyes almost pop out of my head.

"Did you inherit this business?" I ask him after I compose myself.

"No. I built it from the ground up."

"Figuratively speaking?"

"And literally. I built this building too. I took a lot of time to design my own office here too."

"I love it. The design of this office is amazing. The view from these windows is breath-taking. I have never seen anything like it."

"You are breath-taking."

"Pardon?"

Did I hear him right?

"Um… the view. The view is breath-taking," he repeats.

I must not have heard him right. He must have been talking about the view.

"Can you see much inside the other buildings?" I stand at the largest window, looking out of his office.

"At night, you can see a few strange things."

"Like what?"

"Just last week, in that building over there, I saw two people going for it in the office, late at night."

"Going for it?" I smile.

"Yep. Really going for it too. It's quite easy to see people when the lights are on and there are no curtains drawn," he laughs.

"Wow. Public displays of affection aren't really my thing," I laugh.

"So, what is your thing then Karen?"

"Me? I'm really starting to get into appreciating great food."

"Really? I love quality food. It is one of my great passions in life."

"You can't tell. You look so fit."

"Thanks, Karen," his smirks, "But with quality food you don't need a lot of it. You just need enough to appreciate. Where's the best restaurant that you've been to?"

"Down on Flinders St, there is a small place called 'Saki' and it has amazing modern European cuisine."

"Saki? I've never been there. Maybe you'll have to take me there."

"I would love," I look back Russel, "But only if you take me to your favourite restaurant."

"Deal," he states in his strong voice.

"Where is your favourite restaurant then?"

"It's called 'Pierre's.'"

"Pierre's? I'm not familiar with that one. I think I know most of the nice restaurants in our city but I've never heard of that. Where is it?"

"It's in a small town."

"Oh. Ok, where is the small town?"

"In the south of France."

"France?"

"Yes. They make the most amazing 'cuisses de grenouilles'."

"And what are they?"

"Frog legs."

"Frog legs!" I laugh, "I've never eaten frog legs. They don't sound that tasty!"

"Ah, but they are. They are delicious. You'll have to try them when I take you there."

Yes, please – I say to myself as I can't believe the situation. Here I am, with the most beautiful man I have ever seen, and he is inviting me to a restaurant in France. Oh, yes.

Life is good.

"So, Karen how was the first week?"

"Stressful."

"Stressful?"

"Yep. I guess the first week of any job is very stressful," I turn and look back out to the city below his office again, "But when you have a view like this – I guess it eases the stress."

"We can't have you being stressed. You are a valuable member of this team now. Maybe a shoulder rub will help you relax."

I don't agree to it but before I know it, his hands have come up to my shoulders. His hands are amazing, so strong. So manly.

As his strong fingers rub on my shoulders, I feel the tension disappear. He rubs and I start to relax after a hard week of work.

Wow. He is so strong. His touch sends shivers down my spine.

Maybe it's the wine or how smitten I am with him but I turn and kiss him.

He is stunned.

But then, he kisses me back.

Oh yes. His lips are amazing. His touch sends emotions running through me. Wow.

The kiss is so perfect – so emotional.

The moment lasts forever.

But then he pulls away.

"Sorry," he shakes his head and walks out of the room.

Romance: The Billionaire's Assistant

Chapter 3

My weekend is a wreck of nerves.

Have I blown the chance of the job of a lifetime?

It was the most special kiss I have ever experienced but was it worth it? I drink a lot of wine and watch a lot of romantic movies during the weekend, nervous about my next conversation with Russel.

I nervously return to work the next Monday after the kiss expecting to sit down with Russel and explain that the kiss was an accident. It was the end of a big week and there was a lot of stress. I had a sip of wine. I was emotional.

The kiss was a mistake.

Most of all I want to apologise to Russel.

But he does not come in. He 'has' to travel to another city, he tells me via email.

Then he does not come in the next day.

Or the next.

He avoids me and the office for two weeks. During that time, I become increasingly nervous. I have blown it, I admit to myself. I have thrown away the chance at the perfect job. But Russel seems too nice to sack me.

He just keeps avoiding me.

I get the point. He does not want to sack me but he does not want to face me. I have to save him the embarrassment.

I give up the job of a lifetime.

The stress and the nerves are too much and I hand my resignation into the acting office manager, effective immediately.

When I arrive home, I cry.

It seemed like Russel and I were just about to hit it off. I enjoyed working for him and the company. It really was the chance of a lifetime.

And I let it all go for one stupid kiss.

Well – it wasn't a stupid kiss – it was an amazing kiss. It was the most special kiss of my life. When I am old, I will remember that moment. It was incredible. But one kiss doesn't pay the bills.

I start looking for another job right away.

With 'White Property' on my resume, I get another job quickly with another property development firm. But the job isn't as good.

And the boss isn't as good looking.

At the new job, I have to work late hours and I am treated like dirt. I get coffees for chauvinistic males and have to put up with sexual harassment from old men. It seems like this work place is straight out of the 1950's.

After the first week at my new job, I am working late on a Friday night in my small office when there is a knock at my office door.

I answer it, expecting it will be another macho male beating his chest.

But it isn't.

It is the beautiful, handsome, dashing Russel White.

"Hi," I say surprised.

"Hi."

"Hi," I say again.

He smiles with his great smile.

"How are you?" I ask, still standing at the door.

"Good. And you?"

"Good thanks. You?"

He laughs at my obvious nervousness, "Can I come in?"

"Um… yes."

I move some papers off the chair next to my desk to let Russel sit down.

"Looks like they have you working hard? It's nine o'clock on a Friday night and you're the only one left in the office."

"It is hard work. But it's ok. How did you find me?"

"I went to your house first and you weren't home. Your lovely next door neighbour told me you were coming home late every night this week, looking really tired."

"Mrs. Bramble. She always knows what's going on."

"I was hoping that you were late because of work and not a man."

I smile as I sit behind my desk, "Would it have mattered if I was coming home late because of man?"

"Um…," that is the first time I have seen him stumble over his words, "Yes. It would have mattered."

"Really? Why?"

"Um…" he stumbles over his words again, "I guess it doesn't."

"Ok then. So why are you here?"

"I can't let you work for someone else."

"Why not?"

"You know too many of our business secrets."

"Secrets? I was only at your company a few weeks."

"Well, yes. I guess that's not a very good reason then."

"No. It's not. You'll have to come up with something better than that if you want me back in the office."

"I don't want you back in the office," he states bluntly.

"Oh. Ok."

We sit in awkward silence for a few moments.

"Answer me this Russel, why avoid me after that kiss? Why not just come and face me?"

He sighs, "That kiss confused me. I didn't know what to do. My life has always been work, work, work. That is all I have ever known. And I'm good at work. It is a place I can control. To me, dating women was just something I did to fill the time. I had never had a reason not to work. But then I meet you."

His deep, blue eyes look up at me as he continues,

"Right from that first interview, I knew you were amazing. As soon as our eyes connected, I felt something. I couldn't explain it."

"So why was the interview so short?"

He smiles, "My heart rate was racing and I was starting to sweat. You made me nervous. And I'm never nervous. I presented to a conference with over 1000 people and I wasn't that nervous. So that's why I cut the interview short. But after the interview, I couldn't stop thinking about you. Work used to be all I thought about but then it was just you that filled my thoughts. I didn't read that Building Plan paper because I couldn't distract myself from thinking about you."

"Then why run away from the kiss?"

"I was confused. I have never felt like this before. You are the most beautiful person I have ever seen. I need you in my life. Life just isn't enough without you in it."

I melt inside.

He is so perfect.

Again, we sit awkwardly in silence for a few moments.

"I mean, you come back to the office if you like but I would like to take you to dinner first."

"Dinner?"

"Yes. I know a nice little restaurant in France that makes amazing frog legs," he laughs.

"France?" I smile.

"We leave tomorrow morning."

I laugh again, "What about my job here?"

He looks around the messy office, "I'll buy the company out and sack you if you like?"

"No, no need to do that. I'll be happy to leave here."

"Good."

I have to kiss him. I have to let him know that I feel the same.

My heart is in my mouth as I walk around the table. It is beating so hard. My arms are weak with nerves.

I touch his leg.

He looks at me.

Wow. He is so beautiful.

I run my hand up his thigh. His beautiful eyes gaze at me. He understands. I can see the bulge in his pants grow.

He reaches up and kisses me. His lips are so soft, so tender, so juicy. There is passion in the air and the room is alight with chemistry.

As we kiss passionately for a few minutes, my hands run all over his muscular body. But I feel the bugle in his pants press up against me.

"Wait," he whispers, "What if someone catches us?"

"Let them sack me," I reply.

I push him back down onto the seat. I want his manhood in my mouth.

I unzip his pants and his member instantly jumps out like an unleashed tiger. It is so firm.

I put it in my mouth. He is big. And strong. I love it. It tastes like man.

I run my mouth over and over his member and it grows harder with each stroke. He clenches and moans. He is ready to cum.

I pinch the head of his penis with two fingers. He's not going yet. It will not be this quick.

Russel smirks.

Whilst he is seated at on the chair, I pull down my stockings and knickers from under my skirt and he stares in awe. I love his wide-eyed praise.

My skirt is hitched up and I spread my legs over his seated body. He sits ready and hard.

His cock is in my hand and I place my pussy lips at the top of his member. It feels so right. I hold and let my wet pussy juice flow over his strong piece.

I hesitate and he almost explodes in anticipation.

I swallow his hard piece inside me in one go. We both hold our breath in lust. When I move my hips I feel him so deep inside me. I feel every part of his perfectly shaped member inside my pussy.

I am dripping wet.

In the office with my Billionaire. How risky!

I place my finger inside his mouth and his sweet lips lap on my finger as I swivel my hips on the chair.

He moans.

I start to bounce. My thighs push me up and down, and his long member is so hard inside me. I grab the back of his strong neck for support. My other hand reaches behind me and grabs his thigh.

He forcibly unbuttons my shirt and pulls my breasts out of my bra. He nuzzles his face into my breasts, kissing as I bounce.

I squeal.

I feel his warmth squirt inside me and I squeal again.

I stop bouncing and lean forward, resting my head against his chest.

We both take more than a few moments to catch our breath.

I stand off him, taking his member from out of me, and pull on my stockings. He stands, zips his pants and smiles.

Sensational.

"Dinner tomorrow night then?"

"In France?"

"We'll leave in my private jet at midday," he smiles at me again.

Oh yes. What a smile.

What a man.

Romance: Secret Billionaire

Jodi Cooper

Copyright © 2014

Published by Run Free Publishing

All rights reserved.

No part of this publication may be reproduced, stored in a retrieval system, or transmitted, in any form or by any means without the prior permission in writing of the publisher.

Romance: Secret Billionaire

Chapter 1

After another long day at work, I arrive home to my lonely house and spend Tuesday evening cooking dinner for one, sipping at cheap wine. As the lonely night ticks by, I cannot bear the thought of another night spent watching more soppy romantic-comedies.

I am divorced.

I failed at marriage.

Of all the things to fail at, I failed at marriage.

I hate the term – 'failed marriage.' We had a good time once. It was just the good times dried out. And then my ex went looking for good times with someone else.

I hate being lonely.

I feel like it will last forever. I see no end in sight to my loneliest.

I hate it.

Before I know it, the night has gotten late and my bottle of wine has disappeared.

Maybe it will just be this way forever? Just me and my wine.

No.

No, it won't be this way forever.

I have had enough of being the separated lonely woman.

With the confidence that only wine brings, I gather the bravery to order a taxi and travel to the closest bar, where I sit myself down and order a gin and tonic.

It is not long before my bravery starts to pay dividends. A strapping, and dashing, tall man sways next to me.

"Hello."

His demeanour grabs me. He seems nice.

"Hi."

"I'm Bradley."

"Hello Bradley."

He raises his eyebrows while he awaits my response.

"Oh, hi, I'm Jen."

"Hello Jen."

We stand in an awkward silence awaiting for each other to start a conversation.

"Ok. Um… I don't have any ice-breaker conversations. You?" he enquires.

"Nope. I've got nothing."

"Ok," he smiles and turns to leave.

"No, wait. What about we talk about the football?"

"The football?"

"Yeah, the football. It's what all guys want to talk about?"

"Sure, but they probably want to talk about it to other guys. I mean, without football you've got nothing to talk about to other guys. What about shoes? Let's talk about shoes."

"Shoes?"

"All women want to talk about shoes?"

"Probably to other shoe enthusiasts though. Do you love shoes?"

"No, I can't say I do."

"Politics?"

"Too political. What about cars?"

"Too manly."

"The weather?"

"Sure. It's wet today."

"Yes, it is."

We stand in a continued awkward silence.

Then we both burst out laughing.

"How hard is it to strike up a conversation?!" Bradley continues, "Drink?"

"Yes, please."

He confidently orders two martini's, assuming I will drink it, "How do you know I'll drink that?"

"I don't."

"Then why did you order it?"

"There is probably a one percent chance that this is your favourite drink and I'm willing to take that risk."

"It isn't," I smile.

"Drat."

"Drat?"

"Drat. What's wrong with drat?"

"Drat is something a 90 year-old would say once they realise their wheelchair has rolled away. I didn't really expect it from a good looking guy named Bradley."

"Ha!" he laughs nervously, "What should I have said then?"

"The F word would make you look uneducated and the S word would make you look like a hooligan."

"So, you have no advice on which swear would best impress the ladies?"

I laugh, "Some people would be very impressed by a lot of swear words."

"But they're not ladies."

"And I am?"

"Absolutely."

His charm has me captured.

Our drinks arrive and he nods that we should move to a quieter table at the back of the bar.

"You're here alone?" I ask.

"No, I'm here with some friends," he nods in their direction and they are watching us walk to the table, "But you are a lot more interesting."

His cheekiness is disarming.

"What do you do with yourself Jen?"

"Depends if I'm alone or not…"

What?! What did I just say? I tried to be sexy but the look on Bradley's face anything but turned on.

"Right. How about when you're at work?"

"Work, yes," I fumble through my words, "I manage project work at an IT company."

"Sounds respectable."

"It is. You?"

"Builder."

"Really?"

"Yes," his smile catches me again, "Is there something wrong with that?"

"Oh no. Being a builder is great. I just… I didn't expect it from you. You don't look like a builder."

"What do I look like I should be doing then?"

"Banking… no, not banking. Not IT, maybe a teacher."

"Teacher?"

"Well, maybe a Principal or Dean."

"But not a builder? What are builders supposed to look like?"

"A bit rougher than you. You look strong and fit but you don't look like the guy who has a calendar with naked women up on the office door."

"Sure..."

"And you don't look like the guy who wolf-whistles at every girl that walks past."

He wolf-whistles at me, "There. Do you think I'm a builder now?"

"I'm a little more convinced."

I smile at him and he smiles back. This is what chemistry feels like.

"Kids?" I ask.

"Two. Twenty-one and twenty-four."

"Oh. You don't look like you should have children that old?"

"We had our kids young. We thought that would be the best choice family wise."

"We? You're married?"

"If I was still married then I wouldn't be sitting here flirting with you."

"You're flirting with me?" I ask with a raised eyebrow.

"Am I that bad at it?" he looks disappointed, "Sorry. It's been a while."

"Oh no – you're good at flirting! It's me, I'm not very switched on when it comes to guys. I've been out of the game for a while."

"As have I."

"Divorced?" I ask.

What am I doing? What sort of question is that?

"Um... no. The kid's mother passed away eleven years ago. I haven't played the game since."

"Sorry, sorry. I didn't know."

Nice one, genius.

"You're excuse?"

"Found my husband was sleeping with a girl many years younger than me."

"Many years younger than you? That would be mean she would have to be fifteen?" he questions in an obvious attempt at flattery.

"Now that is good flirting. You can tell me that I look young anytime you want," even though it is obvious I am *a lot* older than young.

"Do you have kids?"

"Yes. I have beautiful twin girls, and they just turned 14. They're away at camp for six weeks right now, probably best as I have to sort things out with Chris."

"Chris?"

"Chris is my husband – I mean ex-husband!"

"Sure. I would like to take you out to dinner one day – can I call you?"

"You can call me Jen."

"Uh?"

"It's a joke," he looks at me confused, "Don't worry."

I quickly scribble my number down on a scrap bit of paper before he changes his mind.

He holds out his mobile phone, "The bit of paper is a bit old fashion."

He smiles, puts my phone number in his phone, waves goodbye to his friends and leaves me at the bar.

Have I just been hit on?

Whatever happened, my confidence feels better now. I am aglow. He felt special.

But did he just want sex? Or was it something more?

Romance: Secret Billionaire

Chapter 2

On my train ride to another working day, all I can think about is sex. I took a big risk last night – going to a bar on my own - and yet, here I am, still catching the same train to work every morning.

Sitting on my seat like nothing has changed. But my world feels like it has changed so much. I'm a different person now. But I'm still here, like I was yesterday.

I look around at everyone else and wonder what they are hiding? I am hiding my little adventure from last night but maybe everyone is a little more wild than me?

Has everyone else been part of an underground sex club but no-one has told me? Is everyone else's life as daring as mine?

I wonder what each of the fellow bus riders would be into.

The bus driver, in his mid-fifties, would like to be tied up, I think. He would like to be strung upright and then whipped by a dominant female.

The woman sitting across from me would like to be spanked. I imagine that she would want a stereotypical hunk, a large man with a large package. She would want to be thrown around the room like a ragdoll, spanked with passion.

The tall man at the front of the bus would like dominate people and the young woman standing next to him would like it outdoors.

The soft office boy sitting near the back would like to be taken with a strap-on and the older woman sitting next to him would like to swap partners and have group sex.

How could I have not seen all this before?

Why has no-one else told me that it is normal try new things? I take one risk and suddenly, the world is open to me.

I leave the train for my short walk to work with a smile drenched across my face. After I have ordered my take-away coffee, I see him. Standing tall on the street, his shadow casting long over the ground.

I am smitten.

Wait.

Have I put on enough make-up? How does my shirt ok?

Should I talk to him? Do I ignore him? Do I cross the road and avoid him?

No, too obvious.

Instead I put my head down and pretend to read the news on my phone.

"Jen?"

Dammit.

"Bradley?"

"Hi."

"Hi."

We both seem nervous.

"Um… what are you doing?" He seems as lost as I do.

"Just on my way to work. Drinking coffee," I giggle as I hold my take-away cup aloft.

"Oh right. You work around here?"

"Yep. Two blocks that way."

"Good."

"You?"

"Me? I'm just helping look at some renovations for this building."

"This one?"

"Yep."

"What do they want to do in here? It's quite a large building to redo."

"We've got a few ideas. But there may be some structural problems in what they want to do, so we'll have to look into it a bit further."

"Right."

I feel like a teenager. My voice slightly breaks as I talk to him and I am stricken with nerves.

"Can I buy you a coffee?" he asks.

"I already have one, thanks."

"Right."

We stand in silence.

"Did you want to throw that one in the bin and join me at the café across the road?"

"You don't have work to do?"

"It can wait."

"So, throw this full coffee in the bin?"

"Yeah. Throw it in the bin," he has such a cheeky smile.

"Ok, why not."

"Great."

His smile broadens when I throw the full coffee in the bin and he walks me across the road to sit order coffees. We chat for some time but I am lost in his eyes. I talk on auto-pilot and he smiles beautifully.

Wow.

I could stare at him all day. He's so distinguished. Almost regal.

I blab for a while and when I realise I have said too much I thank him for the coffee.

"Dinner?" he asks.

"It's too early."

"Right. I see. I don't want to rush you into anything."

"I mean in the day," I giggle, "It's too early for dinner."

"Oh, it's a joke."

"Yes. But not very well delivered. I might be interested in dinner. Give me your phone."

He hands me his phone and I type my number in.

"Thanks but I already have your number," he smiles. I am impressed.

"If you can convince me to go to dinner, I'll go," I wink as I leave the café.

Wow, my confidence is so high.

Bradley watches me walk out the door. I turn once outside and he is still watching. What a feeling. That feels amazing.

I fumble through the rest of my week, my mind dreaming about Bradley and his dashing charm. Between work phone calls and meetings, I am smitten. I forget about everything else and just dream about the man. For all my distractions, he is really what has taken my attention.

The smile is so well etched into my face that when I leave to go home for the weekend, it is still there.

When I arrive home to start the weekend, the smiling stops. It's my big, old empty house again. Just me and the emptiness.

Friday nights are the loneliest.

It's the time when it sinks in that my husband has left. My husband left me this big, old lonely house but I'm not sure I want it. It so lonely. So vast and so empty.

I don't like being alone here. There are too many shadows, too many noises. And there's no-one here to protect me.

The wine patches up some of my loneliness. It helps me forget the years I put into that relationship to see him walk out the door. Sometimes it is hard to forget.

Like tonight, when leg of my favourite chair snapped. He would have fixed that. Now the broken chair looks at me like a broken piece of my life.

My husband and I hadn't had sex in many years before we separated.

Before he left, we didn't touch each other for a long time. He was older than me, I'm sure he was starting to struggle to get it up. And when he did, it was weak and small.

I have to stop this. I have to stop feeling sorry for myself and get out of this place.

Everyone tells me that's what I should do.

I look at my phone and search for Bradley's number.

Do I call?

Is that what I want?

I know that I want Bradley but is the relationship what I want?

It's not what I want. I don't want another partner. I don't want another relationship. I don't want to expose myself to that pain again.

I don't want him, do I?

No. I don't.

Surely not already.

I have only been separated for six months.

What is it all about anyway? Why do I feel the need to be attached to a man?

What is it about men that I feel they have to be around all the time. Surely, life is not all about chasing and pleasing men. Surely not.

I could have tried harder with my ex-husband Chris. I should have tried harder with Chris. If nothing for the sake of my children. We should have tried harder.

We owed it to ourselves to try harder.

I look at my phone and Bradley's number. But I flick to my ex-husband Chris's number.

Should we try again?

Can I ever trust him again after what he did to me?

It is moments like this that I want him here. But is it him I want? Or is it just somebody to fill the void that echoes through my house?

Is it missing conversation or is it missing love that makes me feel lonely?

I stare a Chris's number on my phone. I sip my wine. Ex-husband's and wine are probably a bad combination. I place my phone down.

Then I pick it back up and scroll back through to Bradley's phone number. Will he be any better? Will he be an adequate replacement for Chris? Or is it just lust that draws me to him?

I don't know.

How can I know? How can anyone ever know?

I scroll back up to Chris's number. I should call him. I wonder what he's doing right now? Is he as lonely as me? Does he struggle on the Friday nights too?

I should have convinced him to go to counselling. For the sake of our children, I should have convinced him. It would have been worth the effort.

I just don't know if I could have sat there while he made excuses for his mistake. And he would have made excuses. He would have blamed me. Of course he would have blamed me.

He would have said that I did not satisfy him as a wife. He would have said that I could have tried harder.

Maybe I could have tried harder.

Could I?

Or was it him? Or was it us?

No.

What I am saying?

No.

It was not my fault. I did not force his dick down the throat of a younger woman. I did not rub his penis into her pussy. I did not make those choices.

He did.

He could have tried harder.

He should have tried harder.

He should have saved our marriage.

But instead he destroyed it. And I'm the one left with the broken pieces. I'm the one left with a broken chair in an empty house. How could he leave me like this?

And why doesn't he call me? Is he sitting on his couch looking at his phone, waiting for me to call him?

I look at my phone again and scroll through to Chris's phone number. I place my finger up to dial it. But I choose not to. I choose not to call him.

Maybe he is out? Maybe he doesn't want to call me?

He must be out. Drinking with his friends and staring at breasts. They are all the same. All men are the same. All they want is sex. And when they get together, that's all they talk about. I've seen it first hand, the poker nights and the drinking. The laughing and the carrying on.

They are all pricks.

But I miss him.

I miss the way he was here. I could turn around and talk to him. Not that we did talk in the end but there was the opportunity to talk if I wanted to. Maybe counselling could have helped us talk?

I walk over my bookshelf and pull out one of the old photo albums. The twins looked so young then. I sip my wine as I flip through the old memories, trying to remember the love we had for each other. He looked so handsome and I looked so young.

We were in love. In those early days, we couldn't keep our hands off each other. We were smitten with love for each other. I turn to one photo where Chris's eyes are staring at me and filled with such love. He adores me in that photo.

I want that back.

I want that feeling to come back. Where did it go?

I flip through the photos, lost in memories of time gone by. Before long, the bottle of wine is emptied and tears are slowly rolling down my cheeks.

Why did I have to fail at this? Of everything that I could have failed at, why did I have to fail at marriage? I look at Chris's beautiful eyes and I want him back.

I pick up the phone again.

I stare at his number.

I dial.

"Hello."

His voice is hard and full of meanness.

"Hi," I respond.

"I'm busy. Can we talk later?"

The pain comes flooding back.

"Ok."

"Bye."

"Bye."

The call ends and I cry. The pain of our failed marriage is so real. It feels so deep. The pain of his heartlessness grips every part of my body.

What a prick.

What a mean prick.

He is not what I want.

I stop crying.

He is not what I want.

I wipe the tears away.

He is not what I want.

I stand up.

Proud.

I want... what do I want?

What am I craving for after tears, wine and loneliness?

What do I want?

I want a man.

Romance: Secret Billionaire

Chapter 3

The next morning, Saturday, I receive an invite from Bradley for dinner via text.

'Hi. Would love to take you to dinner tonight. Meet at 'Rosemary's' at 9. Bradley Worth."

Wow.

'Rosemary's' is one of the most expensive restaurants in town. He must be trying to impress me. That must be a lot on a builder's wage.

I read the text over and over again. It fills me with confidence. I love the excitement of not knowing what is coming next.

But after reading the magazines about new-age dating, I do something that I swore I would never do. I search his name on Google.

I'm not proud of it – it takes away all the mystery – but I want to know all I can about him.

So, I search the name 'Bradley Worth' in Google.

The first entry is for 'Worth Property and Building'. I click on the website and I quickly realise Bradley is not a builder. His dashing face is splashed on the entrance to the polished website, demonstrating a picture of importance. There are pictures of Bradley with Governors, politicians and sports stars. It becomes apparent that this is not a small business. It is one of the biggest property firms in the state.

I read the company information page and read how Bradley has taken the business from a small one man business twenty years ago, to now one of the biggest building firms in state. He owns property ranging from sports stadiums to high rise skyscrapers.

Wow.

I am impressed.

More than impressed.

I was impressed by Bradley before, but now I am even more impressed.

Why would he hide such a thing?

Why pretend to be a builder when he runs a multi-billion dollar company?

I spend the next hour reading and searching information about the business, astounded at their success, but I keep coming back to Bradley's face, almost addicted to it.

It's not the money I'm interested in, it's the success. He is as driven as I am.

Wow.

Could he be any more perfect?

I patiently wait inside the restaurant, looking around the restaurant for his walk. When I see him walk in, I run my greeting in my head, over and over.

Instead, I ask almost in accusation,

"A builder?"

"Hello."

"You said you were a builder?"

"I am a builder by trade."

"But you run a multi-billion dollar building company?"

"That's a hobby," he sighs.

"A hobby?"

"I still love to be involved. I love building. I love working with my hands."

"That's probably why your company is such a success."

"It wasn't always successful, you know. Hard work goes a long way."

My heart melts.

"Just hard work?"

"And luck. I never dreamt that the company would ever be this successful. I hit the market at the right time, we built a good reputation and then all of a sudden we are the most in demand building company in the state. Then, I invested in the right properties and then – Bang. We hit the right market at the right time."

"Wow…"

"Yeah. It was luck. Probably the new sports stadium is our proudest achievement. It's worth a billion dollars alone."

I am star-struck.

"How was your day?" he asks to break the conversation.

"Nervous."

"Nervous, why?"

"Waiting for now. This is the first real dinner date I've been on in twenty years."

"Twenty years?"

"Absolutely. My husband never even took me to dinner. We never went out. The only time I've been to a restaurant lately is with girlfriends. So, if I start talking about the latest romance novels, please stop me."

He smiles.

"Unless you're into romance novels?" I question.

"Um… no," he responds, "I don't mind the odd romantic-comedy movie but can't say I'm into reading romance novels."

"Good. Because that would be a little strange. Sitting here talking about romance novels to you. Do you read?"

"Since the kids have grown, I've had the time to catch up on some lost reading."

"What do you like to read?"

"Mostly cult classics."

"Such as?"

"Fight Club is a great book. A Clockwork Orange, Gone Girl, The Meaning of Theft – they're all great novels. Reading is such a great way to disappear."

"I love it."

"What do you read?"

"Mostly romance novels. Some erotica," I wink.

"Erotica?" he seems surprised. I sometimes forget that some of the world is stuck in the prudish 2000's.

"It's just romance with some thrills," I smile cheekily. It seems to have gotten his attention.

"What sort of thrills?"

I smile, "It might be better if I show you instead of tell you."

He almost spits out his drink. I've got him – hook, line and sinker.

I can sense his horniness as the waiter delivers the entrees. I knock the shoe off my foot and rub it up Bradley's leg.

His eyes almost pop out of his head.

I can tell that he wants it. I can tell that he is ready to explode.

I grab Bradley's hand.

"You and me. Before the main meals arrive."

"Where?" he responds. I am happy that he knows exactly what I am talking about.

I look around, "The bathrooms?"

"Too obvious. Too many people around."

Wow. I am impressed with his sexual prowess.

"The closest?"

"Too risky."

"The car?"

Bradley does not respond, calculating it over in his head.

"Where is it parked?" I ask.

"The valet parked it in the underground car park."

"Can we get in?"

"We can try," Bradley smiles and grabs my hand, leading me towards my destiny.

We sneak past the two valets at the entrance to underground car park and briskly pace past the cars, looking for Bradley's. Bradley spots it and tugs my hand towards the car.

He unlocks the car and I jump onto the backseat first, pulling down my underwear from under my dress like a horny teenager. He checks the surrounds to make sure there is no movement.

Jumping onto the backseat with the glee of a horny male, he shuts the door behind him, and leaps onto me. We kiss passionately in lust.

Bradley's fingers led up my dress and he touches me. At that moment, I feel something special. This moment is meant to be. Wow.

I moan and bite his ear. Bradley kisses my neck with passion while his fingers enter me. I reach down and loosen his belt, Bradley finishing the undressing by opening his fly and pulling out his member.

I lay backwards onto the seat, spreading my legs wide and ready. Bradley enters me, and slams himself into my wetness. I push against the door of the car, forcing myself closer to Bradley's cock.

A flash of light covers the car.

We both froze in fear.

"Quick, lie down," I whisper.

Bradley lays down on-top of me to hide, his hard penis still inside me. The flashlight again flashes over the car, "It's the valet."

"What's he looking for?"

"We were probably making too much noise," Bradley smiles.

We hear the footsteps of the valet come closer, the light shining over our car.

"Shhh…" Bradley giggles.

The footsteps pass.

We both expel a sigh of relief as the footsteps and light go into the distance.

"Now, where were we?"

Bradley begins to pump me again, "Oh yes, there it is."

Bradley slides under me, and I straddle him on-top. I jump on his cock, coming in the process. I lean forward to catch my breath, but Bradley begins to pump upwards.

I moan loudly as Bradley cums inside me.

We catch our breath.

The flashlight comes closer again.

"Quick, get dressed," I whisper.

I leap off Bradley, pulling back on my knickers. Bradley quickly does up his pants as the footsteps come closer again.

As the flashlight shines on our car, we both leap out the side door.

"Evening," Bradley states to the valet, within a few feet of our car.

"Is this your car?" he questions.

I begin to giggle, and Bradley responds "Yes, this is our car. We just forgot our… our… um… just forgot our purse. But you have it now, don't you darling?"

I hold my purse aloft for the valet.

"Ok, just do your hair up before you head back into the restaurant," the valet smiles.

As the valet turns, we struggle to hold in our giggles. When the valet is in the distance, we both burst out laughing.

"What a good a dinner this is," we laugh.

Romance: Secret Billionaire

Chapter 4

It is only a few short days before I meet Bradley for dinner again and we have dinner at a restaurant around the corner from my house.

"How is work?" I ask.

"Good. I was a little distracted though."

"Distracted? Why?"

He shrugs his shoulders, "I might have been thinking about this amazing lady that I have met."

"Tell me more…"

"Well, she has wonderful eyes, beautiful hair, an amazing smile and a great personality."

"She sounds amazing."

He smiles.

Then it the silence turns uncomfortable.

"I'm talking about you," he states.

"Oh, good," I breathe a sigh of relief.

"It has been a while since I've met someone like you. I've always told my son that you should never chase women, the right one will just come along one day. And he always asked how you know she is the right one."

"And what did you say?"

"Nothing. I would always just smile at him and nod. Because you never can tell. Feelings can't be predicted. Somebody might seem right but the chemistry is lacking. Or somebody might be all wrong but the chemistry is perfect."

"I agree, one hundred per-cent. You can't predict how you're going to feel when you meet someone."

He nods.

"I've been distracted at work too," I mention.

"And what has kept you distracted?"

"Well, I've met this guy. He is wonderful, charming, handsome and has such an amazing personality."

He looks around, looking for the person I'm talking about.

"Me?" he questions cheekily.

"Yes - you."

He leans across the table and kisses my lips gently. I am swept away.

He then sits back down with a smile from ear to ear.

We talk and talk and talk.

He listens so well and he converses greatly.

Yes.

This is what I want.

We talk long into the night about nothing. We could be talking about the price of bread but it doesn't matter, we just love talking to each other.

I am so smitten and so glad that we found each other.

He tells me that he is so happy that we meet and I tell him how happy that life turned out this way.

Wow.

Of all the new experiences that I have felt over the past few weeks, this is the most amazing. The feeling of being infatuated by a man. I could listen to him talk all day, I could stare at his face all night.

When it is late, he offers to walk me home.

We wander down the street and I feel safe and secure. I don't feel vulnerable and I don't want to.

Yes. This is what I want.

Walking up to my house, I see a shadowy figure on the front step.

No.

Not now.

I grip Bradley's hand tighter as we approach.

"What are you doing here Chris?"

"Who's he?" Chris states firmly.

"None of your business. I asked you not to come back here."

"This is still my house. And who are you?" this time Chris asks Bradley directly.

"I should go," Bradley states.

"No Bradley, my ex-husband is just leaving."

"Ex?" Chris questions, "I'm no ex. We're still married."

"We're separated Chris. I've signed the divorce papers."

"I don't want to be separated anymore. That's why I'm here, I want us to try."

"You made your choice Chris."

"It was the wrong choice. I made a mistake. One mistake shouldn't why we throw away all those years we had together," he pleads.

"Just because we were together doesn't mean it was good. We're not doing this now Chris. Not here."

"I won't let you walk into this house with that thing," he nods to Bradley.

"I am no thing, my name is Bradley," he is stoic, proud.

"Whatever. Just walk away like the little boy that you are."

Bradley is stunned at Chris's rudeness. But the rudeness doesn't surprise me, I've had too many years of it.

"I am no boy," Bradley does not back down and Chris brings to fire up.

"I will beat you like a little boy," Chris, as always, follows his talk with the threat of physical violence.

Bradley, who stands taller than Chris, stands his ground.

"I think you'd better leave Chris."

"Leave? Are you joking? I'm not going anywhere," he steps towards Bradley.

To Chris's surprise, Bradley continues to stand his ground.

"Well…" Chris tries to intimidate Bradley.

Bradley stands tall.

There is a brief moment of confusion for Chris, for years he threatened me with physical violence and I had no response but to give in. Now, I have a saviour.

Chris, with the emotional intelligence of a twelve year old, walks away,

"Watch yourself, boy. Watch yourself."

I watch as Chris aggressively screeches his car up the street in defeat and I whisper to my hero,

"Sorry."

Bradley smiles,

"There's nothing to be sorry for."

We stand in complete silence for more than a few moments until he nods towards the entrance to my house,

"I could sure use that drink now."

Smiling, I know I have made the right choice.

Bradley or Chris?

Years of nothing or a life full of love?

I choose what is right for me, right now.

Lust, love, desire and commitment.

I choose to be me.

I choose Bradley.

Bonus Story

Romance: Bad Boy Biker

Jodi Cooper

Copyright © 2014

Published by Run Free Publishing

All rights reserved.

No part of this publication may be reproduced, stored in a retrieval system, or transmitted, in any form or by any means without the prior permission in writing of the publisher.

Romance: Bad Boy Biker

Chapter 1

I haven't seen Maggie in ten years.

We were best friends in college but after college our lives went very different paths. We tried to keep in contact but our worlds became too busy and full. She was attracted to the slower pace of life and went off to live in a small town in the middle of the country, while I chased the big dollars in a bustling city. We knew that when we said our goodbyes ten years ago that our lives would take very different directions.

I love the city. I love the hustle and bustle, the fever of doing, and the electric atmosphere of millions of people. I love the shopping and bars, the pace and excitement. You couldn't take me away from the city. I'm addicted to it. Maggie was always different to me. She loved the easier lifestyle and the chance to be in everyone's business.

She reached out to me via the internet. She wanted to have a party to celebrate her divorce, so how could I say no?

I have come down the day before the divorce party, eager to catch up over old times before we celebrate. I am to meet her at the bar that she works at - after driving many, many hours.

As I drive up to the bar, I become nervous. The night is dark but the bar is darker. There are lines and lines of tough motorbikes parked outside. And if it isn't a motorbike, it's a truck.

Three men with ripped black t-shirts watch my new city car drive into the car park.

"Hello honey!" they laugh as my feet step out of the car.

If I thought my car looked out of place, I quickly realize that my tight black skirt is even more out of place.

I clutch my purse tightly as I ignore their statements and walk into the rowdy bar – it's full of loud music, loud people and loud drinking. The place is a bubble of action. It is packed full of boisterous customers, each group yelling louder to be heard over each other and the music.

Tattoos adore most of the people around me. I must really look out of place.

I walk in and look behind the bar for Maggie. I can't see her but a lot of people have taken a liking to me. This place is starting to scare me.

"Sarah!" Maggie grabs me unexpectedly from behind and gives me a great big hug, "So great to see you!"

I hug her back, more for security than longing.

"Um… crazy place you work in," I almost have to yell in her ear for her to hear me.

She winks, smiles her cheeky smile, grabs my hand and walks me towards the end of the bar. We arrive at what appears to be the quiet end of the bar, it is almost protected from the noise around the corner of brick wall.

"This is the regular's part of the bar. It's a little quieter than out there," Maggie smiles.

"Nice place."

Maggie shrugs her shoulders, "It pays the bills. You'd be surprised – on a night like this, I can get some great tips. The drunker they get, the more they tip. Everyone's a winner."

I always loved Maggie's positive outlook, she would always find the upside to every situation.

"It's so good to see you!" she smiles again, "How's life in the big city?"

"You know, it's exciting but nothing exciting happens. How's life in the small town?"

"You know, it's slow but nothing exciting happens," she laughs, "You got a big city man?"

I shake my head, "They come and go, but no-one worth running after. They never fit my long list of credentials. You got yourself a small city man?"

"No, but who needs a man when you've all this?!" she laughs again.

I shake my head. After all these years apart, she has barely changed a bit. She might have aged a few days but she is still smiling, still seeing the world through rose-tinted glasses.

I used to be like that.

But not anymore. Maybe it's the big city that has gotten to me but I'm a lot more cynical now than when I was in my college days.

"You still looking for love? Still looking for that man in shining armour?" she asks, in reference to my college dreams of being swept away by the perfect man.

"The perfect man doesn't exist. He is just an ideal – a hope. All these city men, they might be good looking but they don't know how to change a tyre let alone fix a door. I need someone tough but educated."

"So you haven't found your perfect man in the city?"

"Nope. And I'm sure I won't find him here."

She smiles again, "Thanks for coming out. It's so great to see you. Let me serve one more round at the bar and then we can go back to my place and catch up."

"What?" I whisper through clenched teeth, "You're going to leave me here by myself?"

"Oh relax. Just sit tight for ten minutes and don't talk to any strangers."

Damn.

Maggie leaves our end of the bar and walks back out into the madness and noise to serve more drinks, leaving me alone in the roughness. I'd run off to the toilets to hide but the women in those toilets are probably as scary as it is out here.

Instead, I sit at the bar and wait nervously, looking straight into my drink.

"She a friend of yours?" a deep, strong voice asks next to me.

I don't want to look at whoever it is.

And I definitely don't answer.

"Not talking uh?"

Again, I don't answer.

"You're not from around here then?"

I turn and look at the deep, strong voice.

Oh.

Wow.

He is stunning. Strong, square jaw with beautiful, tanned skin. His muscles bugle from under his tight black shirt, and his strong arms are covered by tattoos.

He looks straight ahead while I study him. His hair is messy and his face is unshaven. He has a scar above his right eye, and a thick, tough body.

Perfect.

"Um…" I stutter.

He looks at me with beautiful eyes, "New to town?"

"Maggie told me not to talk to strangers," I smile nervously.

"Maggie shouldn't talk to strangers," he laughs, "That girl gets herself into too much trouble. I'm Lance."

He holds out his large hand to shake mine, and when our hands touch, I feel shivers run through my body. The skin on his hand is rough, like it has experienced years of hard work.

"Pleased to meet you, Lance. I'm Sarah."

"How do you know Maggie?"

"We're old friends. We went to college together. She moved out here after college and I went off to the work as a lawyer in a large firm in the city."

He nods slowly.

"Maggie was brave letting you come out here by yourself on a Friday night."

"Is this place trouble on a Friday night?"

"This place is trouble every night. But you can guarantee there'll be trouble on a Friday night. And beautiful girls like yourself don't belong in bars where there's trouble."

Charming as well as rough. Hmmmm.

"And what sort of trouble can I get myself into?"

He looks at me, "Just watch out. Trouble will find you."

His voice sends emotions streaming through my body. He is so perfect in every way.

"Sarah," Maggie interrupts my dreaming, "I thought I told you not to talk to strangers."

Lance smiles and moves away from the bar as soon as Maggie arrives.

I watch his cute bottom and broad shoulders walk away from me and out into the madness. The crowd moves out of his way as he walks through.

"Who was that?" I ask, obviously impressed.

"That was Lance. Stay away from him, he is trouble."

"Funny. He said the same thing about you."

"Yeah, well, I haven't been to jail. Lance has."

I try to look for him again amongst the crowd but he has vanished.

Romance: Bad Boy Biker

Chapter 2

After Maggie has signed off from her shift behind the bar, she grabs my hand with a smile on her face.

"Time to catch up," she laughs as we start our walk outside, "Just don't make eye contact with anyone as we leave."

We walk out of the noise through a side door, and into the dimly lit staff car park.

"Shit."

"What's wrong?"

"Just keep your head down and don't say a word," she whispers.

"What's wrong?" I ask again.

"Those four men," she states quietly, pointing to four dark shadows near the cars, "They're real trouble. They've been banned from the bar a few times."

"Well, should we go get someone to escort us to the car?" I ask.

Maggie looks at me, "No. We're tough. Just don't say anything to them."

As we get closer to Maggie's car, we are approached by the four large shadows.

"Hello girls."

"Piss off," Maggie is firm.

"Ooohhh, I like them rough."

"Take your fat arse and go home," Maggie starts to get aggressive.

"Now, now. Let's not be too feisty. We just want to get to know you girls better."

The voice is old and creepy, and it drives shivers through me.

We almost make it to the car when one of them grabs Maggie's arm. Maggie instinctively swings with her other arm and hits him flush on the face. He is a taken aback but not sore.

"You bitch," he states as he wipes the blood from his nose.

Suddenly, all four of them are around us. One grabs me from behind, wrapping his arms around my chest. I try to struggle but he is strong. He squeezes me tight as another walks in-front of me. All I can see is the broken, creepy smile on his face.

I feel defeated. Helpless. I close my eyes because I don't want to see what happens next.

But suddenly, the one holding onto to me let's go and falls to the ground. When I open my eyes I see the one in-front of me fall, smashing onto the concrete.

I watch as a large dark shadow grabs the two men holding Maggie and throws them to the ground as well. A few punches fly from the large shadow and the four men whimper in retreat.

The large shadow stands strong with wide shoulders, as our protector, and the four men scurry out of the car park.

Wow.

As the shadow turns around and walks towards us, I realize it is Lance.

"You ok?" he asks, in his deep voice.

I nod nervously.

He looks at Maggie.

She nods too.

He provides a small smile and then I watch in awe as he walks back into the bar.

Romance: Bad Boy Biker

Chapter 3

We arrive at Maggie's without saying another word, still shaken by our earlier incident.

Once inside her house, Maggie knocks open a beer, sculls it, and then says, "Sorry, Sarah. I should have known someone like you would have gathered attention in that bar. I shouldn't have asked you to come out there. That was silly of me."

"Oh no, don't worry about it," I try to brush it off, "If this was the city, everyone would have just shot each other with handguns."

We laugh a nervous laugh.

"Drink?" she asks.

"Please."

She pours two scotch's and hands me one, before sculling hers.

"What would have happened if Lance didn't come?"

"Don't think about that, Sarah. It didn't happen, so don't think about it. It's a dangerous place, that bar, and if you were to think about everytime you come close to trouble, you'd stress yourself out."

"Have you ever been in more trouble than that?"

"No. That's the worst I've seen it. I'll tell my boss tomorrow and he'll make sure those guys don't trouble us again."

"Why do you work there? It's so dangerous."

"You know, it's not usually as bad as that. On the weeknights, it's a great place to work. It's quieter and the people give you a lot of respect. You have a laugh with your regulars, and the other staff are great. But the weekend is when the money comes in. The weekends are where the money is made because all the out-of-towners come in and splash their cash on getting drunk."

"So it's the money versus safety?"

She nods.

"We were lucky Lance was there," I mention.

"We were lucky."

"Maybe I should go back and thank him?"

"Thank Lance? No way, Sarah. That man is dangerous. He is pure danger."

"He saved us from danger though."

"Those guys would have only been there because they were looking for Lance. They weren't waiting for us, they were waiting for Lance. He's dangerous."

"Why is he so dangerous?"

"Trouble follows him. Everywhere he is, trouble is. He gets in fights all the time. And he's always the one that wins the fights."

"Really?"

"You quite often see him fighting three or four guys at once. He's strong and tough. And rough."

"Hmmm…" I show my satisfaction.

"Sarah, I've warned you. You should stay away from him. He isn't a city type, he's all country and rough."

I nod and scull my drink too. That brings a smile to Maggie's face and she pours another drink.

We start to relax and forget about our moment of terror, talking about our separate lives and reminiscing about our time a college.

As we talk, Maggie drinks. She has drunk eight drinks by the time I have finished my second. She mentions that the drinks help her calm her nerves, and as tough as she is, I can see that our incident tonight has shaken her up.

She was always able to drink a lot at college but her drinking has gotten better from living out here.

After Maggie has drunk many drinks to calm the raging adrenalin and nerves, she falls asleep on the couch, slumped into the cushions. Having only had two glasses of scotch, I grab a blanket and cover her up. I then sneak around to find her keys and head back outside back to the car.

I have to go back and thank Lance. He saved me from the worst moment possible. I have to say thanks to him, even though Maggie has warned me not too.

Maybe it's the adrenalin or the scotch, but I drive Maggie's car back to the seedy bar. My hands shake nervously at the wheel as I think about the danger in the bar. After parking in the dimly light car park, I hop out and am greeted by a chorus of sexist remarks.

"Hello legs!"

"Bring that skirt over here, lovely!"

"Show us your tits!"

I ignore them and walk straight to the entrance.

It has gotten rowdier.

It's nosier and busier. Men and women are packed in and are bumping their way through each other. My petite body squeezes in the gaps and heads towards the regular's spot. I look for my saviour, Lance, but I cannot see him. I look to where he was seated earlier, but he has gone.

Oh no.

What I have I done?

I felt safe with Lance around but now I'm alone in the rowdiest bar I have ever seen. I feel a hand rest on my pert bottom and I turn around to see a large biker smiling at me. I quickly move away and hide amongst some other people. Luckily, he moves on.

My heart rate is now in my mouth. I now have to try to get back to the car by myself. I can't stay here and wait for Lance to show up, this place is too dangerous. I consider hiding in the toilets until morning but it is probably just as dangerous in there.

I'm scared.

I feel another strong hand rest on my shoulder.

Shit.

"I thought you would have had enough of this place."

Turning, I see Lance. He stands tall, strong and powerful.

I breathe a long sigh of relief.

"Um... I just came back to say thankyou."

"Thankyou?"

"Yeah, thankyou for stopping those guys before."

"Oh, sure. That was no problem. I don't like them anyway."

We stand in awkwardness for a few moments.

Right.

I'm here. I've said thankyou. Now what?

Be brave.

Going on instinct, my hand reaches out and lands on his crotch. I hold it there, cupping the large package in his jeans.

His eyes almost pop out of his head.

"No, really," I say, "I want to thank you."

He looks confused. But quickly that confusion is taken over by a charming smile.

He grabs my hand and leads me to the back of the bar, where there is a door that has a sign reading 'Staff Only'. Lance plays with the handle but it is locked. He looks around, and after not seeing any staff members, he slams his strong shoulders into the door. The door breaks open with the force of this man. Again he grabs my hand and leads me in.

Oh yes.

It is a small office, dimly lit by a light hanging from the ceiling. He shuts the door behind us and tries to lock it but it won't stay shut. Instead he uses his strength and pushes the heavy desk in-front of the door, to prevent anyone barging in.

Oh yes.

His muscles bugle through his shirt as he heaves the desk into place. He is so powerful.

Yes.

Once the large desk is in place, he turns back to me.

"I'm glad you came back," his deep, manly tone sends shivers through my body, "You have the most beautiful eyes I have ever seen."

Rough and charming. Perfect.

As he approaches me, I start to question my decision. Is this really the best choice? Should I really be in this office with a complete stranger? I think about leaving but then Lance rips off his shirt.

Wow.

He is muscular and toned, his shoulder muscles rippling as he throws his shirt to the side. His strong chest bugles outward and his stomach is flat and ripped.

I can't resist a man that looks like that.

His large hands rest on the sides of my shoulders and he leans in and kisses me. For all his strength, his lips are so tender. So delicate.

Damn it. I can't say no.

As he kisses me again, I feel like a piece of meat that is about to be used for Lance's servicing pleasure.

And I like it.

He kisses my neck, pulling my hair to the side.

I like it a lot.

How did this happen so quickly? How I am in this small office with this beautiful biker? Wow, he must be confident.

He kisses my shoulder and it sends shivers through me. I kiss back at his neck.

Oh, he smells so good. He smells like I thought he would. He smells like man. Yes.

As I rub my hands over his body, I become primal. I know where I am and what I want. This man's body is a piece of artwork. I can't ignore it any more.

I tear the jacket off my back and throw it on the floor. My hands rub all over his toned and muscular body. My hands smooth up his toned arms and around his shoulders. I run my hands down his solid chest as he kisses me. I try to push against his chest but it is so hard.

Oh yes – he is so muscular.

He takes control.

He pulls off my skirt and my underwear in one clean movement, and continues to undress himself. As his jeans go down, so do I. I yank down his jocks and expose his large manhood. Oh yes.

He is big. And solid.

I put him in my mouth and bounce my head up and down his shaft. He moans. My lips lap around his solid manhood, smoothly running up and down his cock. I start to bounce my head and the faster I bounce my head, the louder he moans. Yes – he is shouting for more. I love it.

He pulls me up by the shoulders and throws my naked body onto the desk like a doll. I am so wet, I want him inside me.

He guides his member towards my pussy, and slides in. Oh yes – I have the world's best looking biker inside me. Oh yes.

I feel him push deep inside me - he is stretching at the width of my lips – and he begins to thrust. I rub my hands up and down his arms – I want to eat him all up.

He is amazing.

He thrusts me harder, pumping his member into me.

He brings my legs up to his shoulders and as his hips thrust into me, his arms pull my legs back down. Oh yes.

He jams me with force and I try to grip the table's edge to hold still. His member is reaching me in places that haven't been touched before. I become hot, and I start to shake.

Wow.

I run my hands up to his manly chest and it is everything I ever wanted. It is so toned and hot. So strong. He pumps and pumps me.

Yes!

He withdraws and aggressively turns my body over, leaning me forward over the table. I poke my wet pussy out for him and he quickly finds the spot. Oh yes, he finds the spot.

Wow.

He smashes his hardness into me, driving my hips into the table. I try to push back against him but he is so strong. I feel his hands run all over my back, and then they grab the flesh of my behind, pulling at it. He slaps me. Oh yes.

I listen to him groan with aggression. He continues to slam into me, pumping into the table. I quickly orgasm. As my body temperature soars through the roof, I hold onto the table and he jams again. He is so strong. He pumps me one last time.

Wow.

When he withdraws he slumps to a nearby chair. I roll over on the table and stare at the roof.

"Oh yes," I puff, "What a moment."

We lie in the orgasmic rush of passion for more than a few minutes until reality starts to set back in. We move from our positions and fumble through our clothes on the floor. I am shaking as I pull up my skirt. I struggle to walk and realise that I am going to be sore tomorrow.

After we get dressed, I wonder what is next for us, but Lance jumps in first.

"Beer?" he asks.

"I don't think I should go back out there. But I might need an escort to my car."

"You're not driving that car anywhere," he smirks.

He grabs my hand, pushes the table out of the way and leads me through the loud busy bar. We walk out the front doors where he leads me to his tough, rough bike.

I look up at him and he smiles his charming smile. He starts the bike with a roar, and I climb on the back. I grip his solid body and we power away on the back of his motorbike with an aggressive growl.

Perfect.